Maurice Leitch was born in the North of Ireland in 1933 and worked as a schoolteacher for some years before joining the BBC as a Features Producer.

His first novel, *The Liberty Lad*, was followed by *Poor Lazarus*, which won the Guardian Fiction Prize in 1969, and in 1975 he published *Stamping Ground*.

Silver's City was the winner of the 1981 Whitbread Prize.

Maurice Leitch

SILVER'S CITY

First published in Abacus 1983 by
Sphere Books Ltd
30–32 Gray's Inn Road, London WC1X 8JL

Copyright © 1981 by Maurice Leitch

First published in Great Britain 1981 by
Secker & Warburg Ltd

'Stand by Your Man' (Tammy Wynette/Billy Sherrill)
copyright © 1968 Al Gallico Music Corp. (USA)
sub-published by Keith Prowse Music Publishing Co Ltd
Reproduced by permission of EMI Music Publishing Ltd,
138–140 Charing Cross Road, London WC2H 0LD

Reproduced, printed and bound in Great Britain by
Hazell Watson & Viney Ltd, Aylesbury, Bucks

For Dan and Sandra

The Devil hath established
His cities in the North

St Augustine

1

THEIR CAR CONTINUED cruising softly along tree-lined avenues, and a fog horn blew its plaintive note somewhere off to the right. They were in one of the better parts of town, deep greens and gardens backing almost to the water's edge, lawn-mowers silent now, cooling in the dark. And inside, thought Galloway, all those happy families.

In the reflected glow of the dash, Duff and Tweed – Galloway had said all they needed was a stage act – watched him smiling to himself, and they were a little afraid, as always, of this cold fish. Halfway along the Somerton Road, the driver, Tweed, perhaps because of that fear, made a sharper left turn than was necessary, and the Cortina stalled. Duff, who was in the back seat, came forward sharply, and his breath, sweet and rank with the rum he had been drinking most of the day, seemed to fill the enclosed space. Galloway glanced at him and he moved back, sighing, into the recesses.

Once more they crept ahead under near-interlocking boughs.

One of Galloway's fancies was of a *daytime* rampage through such quiet reaches. All the pickings were here, he told himself, not in their own sooty environs. They were city rats; here lived a plumper, more domesticated species. Behind him, Duff was going through his pockets again, a compulsion, Galloway noted, he now carried over into his everyday life.

"Are you sure," he enquired sweetly, "you've got it?" although he knew the irony would be wasted. Then, "Put it away, Duff, put it away," as he saw the proffered butt of the Walther, and the other's damp, eager face in the mirror.

A smell of gun-oil assailed their nostrils. Galloway hated to be reminded so insistently of what he was about. It took away any twist of the unexpected, something he enjoyed deeply, watching himself meet it, head-on, strong, arrogant, dangerous. These heavy fools he was given to work with, they ate up a man's patience. Earlier tonight, for instance, the number of times their route had been traced out on a street map, as if by touch some voodoo might make their mission all that easier. He didn't want it made easy.

"Take the next avenue to the right," he told Tweed. "We're almost there."

He rolled the window down, and the air was crisp. It was September, there was a smell of burning. How easy they have it, these punters, he thought. The way it is on the television commercials, for that's how he pictured them at number forty-four. Only – he looked at his watch – in about two minutes from now, that cosy domestic scene was going to change dramatically.

"Now, listen," he said. "When I say pull up, do it – but easy. Got it?"

Tweed nodded, squinting in concentration. A short-sighted driver, thought Galloway. Marvellous.

Duff said, "There's a street-lamp outside the house." He sounded alarmed.

"Sure there is. And that's why friend Tweed here is going to park the car when and where I tell him to. Aren't you, Tweed?"

They idled past. Lights on in only one of the top front windows – a bedroom – all dark downstairs; so no parties, no visitors.

"Right. Here." A pause. "Now, switch off."

They both looked at him. "We're not in fucking Chicago," he said. Tweed cut the engine.

"Now, let's have it."

2

Duff handed the piece across the seat into Galloway's gloved hand. By the weight, he knew it held its full clip of eight. He checked the safety catch.

"Okay," he said. "Don't touch the starter until I come back out through the gate. You can have the door open, if you want."

They both said, "Okay, Ned," in a rush, first time anyone had used his christian name that night. It made him feel clammy, that sort of thing always did. Although he wore gloves, he still wiped the butt of the automatic on his handkerchief before slipping it inside his flying jacket.

Ned Galloway got out of the car and began walking at an even pace back towards the lamp. The night was calm with just a hint of chill in the air. Bonfires of dead leaves had been lit in several of the back gardens. An evening for a stroll, except he was the lone walker on this long white avenue. A night for courting couples, hand-in-hand. Stars out, too. The pattern was a familiar one, the way details were starting to flood in.

He reached the gate – wrought metal – and it opened with barely a sound. There was a child's plastic bucket lying in the middle of the path, and beyond it an overturned tricycle. Careless with their belongings, these people. The others in the car were given to describing them as slapdash, as a race; no amount of money or position could ever disguise it, they asserted. Galloway had little time for such theories. To him it was just another instance of talking shit for its own sake.

He edged the zipper of his jacket down towards his belt, for greater ease of movement when the time came, then put his finger on the bell and moved back as the muffled chimes pealed inside. Once would be enough, he could tell. He felt cool and perfectly calm. And that other sensation too, he recognised, as though there were two of him, the other, some little way off, noting each move he made – giving points as well, it always seemed to him, like stars in class for performance.

The door opened and a girl of ten or so faced him. "Yes?" she said. She had a book in her hand, one finger marking the place. He could even read the title, *Living Things of the Sea-Shore*.

Galloway said, "Is the doctor in? There's been a bad car accident," motioning back towards the road. There was no drama in his voice. She would remember it later; that, and his accent. The single earring too. Kids got everything right, not like their elders, who, from Galloway's reading of the papers these days,

3

seemed to be half-blind as well as deaf. This little number in the green gymslip would be spot-on, he reckoned.

"Could you hurry, please. It's a matter of life and death."

That got to her, he could see. She had blonde pigtails, he also noted, and knickers in the school colours, as she raced up the stairs two at a time, her book of pictures flying. He hoped she would stem her curiosity and stay up there, for he liked cool little numbers like this one. He used to enjoy watching them on the top of buses in the afternoons.

"Daddy! Daddy!" she was crying out somewhere at the top of the stairs.

Ned Galloway took out his handkerchief and wrapped it about his left hand, then let it drop limp, the sort of detail that singled him out from the other cowboys ranging the streets on stolen wheels. Now he waited, stance easy but controlled. His mind felt empty. Practice makes perfect, he told himself.

The man appeared near the head of the stairs, jacket in one hand, bag in the other. He put it down on the carpeted tread and stooped to peer at Galloway under the lintel. Galloway moved forward into full view, keeping his bandaged hand forward.

"A crash, you say?"

Galloway pointed, as he had done before. The man came down one more step. "Are you hurt yourself?" he asked. Galloway had forgotten that trick doctors have of looking straight at you in that way of theirs.

"Not too bad," he answered. The words sounded foolish. He had forgotten, as well, hadn't he, how the quack always likes to make you feel stupid.

But now Galloway was impatient to finish his task. He said, "Could you please hurry, Doctor Delargy," and that was a mistake, for the man's eyes changed.

"Who are you?" he said. "How do you know my name? Where do you want me to go?"

Galloway moved forward into the hall, his right hand dipping inside his open jacket. "Nowhere," he said. "This will do nicely," and the weapon came into view.

The man above stared at his bandaged hand moving the safety catch, then he turned and began scrambling back up the stairs. He was panting and falling, as if the carpet had become slippery. Galloway's first bullet hit him in the upper part of the legs, yet he continued sculling with his arms. He didn't cry out, Galloway noted, but just went on clutching at the banisters. A rage came over Galloway. They would never allow you the satisfaction of submitting cleanly. He raced up the stairs, mounting their soft treads, and, at close range, poured three more shots into his victim's back and neck. Warm blood stippled the gun and the hand that held it. He looked down at the bright freckles, like paint. His skin stung, as if he was wounded.

In the hallway, he turned. The girl was screaming now, all right. Her cries seemed to come from behind a closed door. It couldn't be explained – that, and the way his hand burned. He looked down at it curiously, turning it over and over, and from side to side. He couldn't get the idea out of his head that the man on the stairs had managed to strike back at him in some way. He stared at the heap on the stairs, looking for answers. Old enough to be his father, a bit of a paunch, one hairless leg, bare to the knee. There was a flattened blob of chewing gum on the heel of his right slipper. He had come down to him wearing those.

At the door, Galloway was sure he heard a movement, then something whispered. "Mistake," it sounded like, but they all said that.

Then, in the middle of it all, he suddenly heard another sound, the car engine, and not just the quiet cough into life of the motor, either, but a revving, vicious and impatient. Galloway began to run down the path, pulling the handkerchief from his fist as he went. The garden gate flew back at his passing, and now he was sprinting for those twin red lights. They seemed to quiver like something waved gently to mock, suspended in the evening mist. He saw the white fume of the exhaust – further mockery. He would take a terrible toll for this, he promised himself.

So, he was running hard along this dead, suburban avenue, and making no sound because of his plimsolls, when, for no reason, it seemed at first, he began slowing down. The car with its frantic engine was still a good thirty yards off – they had spotted him – yet he broke his stride until he was merely strolling. The word itself seemed somehow to have its own calming effect. *Strolling*. He said it to himself. "Just taking a stroll." It had come over him like a net dropping. Then – why not, he asked himself, for he couldn't be touched. Not by anyone. Least of all, by any of *them* out there, listening and holding their breath behind locked doors. *They* pay for all of this, he told himself. Any price they'll pay, not to be disturbed.

He listened and looked, but nothing moved. No doors opening, no lights off or on, no voices. The warm gun was still in his hand. He moved it slowly about, although there was no threat. A car backfiring, they'd say later, that's what it sounded like. If they would say anything.

He walked to the car, taking his time, but, before he reached it, he stopped for a last look along the row of sleeping villas. Trees and lawns and a thick stillness that could only be bought with lots of cash. To show them that they were still only bunnies in his, Ned Galloway's, book, he did a singular thing. The two in the car watched with incredulity – or, rather, Tweed the driver, did; Duff was being sick over the floor of the car at this time, having no stomach, in every sense, for any more. Through the rubbed oval in the rear window, Tweed watched Galloway crouch and bring together gloved hands, in that firing stance he'd only ever seen in films before. The gun swung, searching for a target along the darkened fronts of the houses, a hint of life anywhere – but there was none. Neither of them, it seemed, had noticed the few remaining lights go out. Such slyness enraged Galloway. The last rounds he had in his clip he pumped at the only illumination left, the street-lamp some yards off. Its glow burst with satisfying detonation, raining glass almost at his feet and on the hedges and clipped grass. Let them find it there tomorrow, he thought, when the mowers crunch over it. And the headless iron standard, another memento.

Meanwhile, in the car, Tweed still looked on aghast. Such behaviour was beyond him. Stories about that one out there, legs apart in that cowboy fashion, hadn't prepared him for any of this. He was a family man; that's where he should be now, he told himself. He shivered. Drink and drinking had driven him to volunteer for this night's work, but it had all turned out to be like a bad dream. Or, in the words of the younger lads, a bad trip. Could this Galloway character be "high" – another expression of theirs?

As if to present himself for inspection, the man outside on the road at that moment turned his face towards the rear window. He was smiling and he brought the gun up until it was trained on Tweed's pale mug. His finger tightened, Tweed dropped, there was a click, for the magazine was empty – although the man in the car was not to know that.

Galloway strode to the front passenger door, then tapped the glass politely. He felt purged, and so could relax now with head back on the seat, eyes closed, and let the car take him where it would.

2

LATER THAT SAME NIGHT, in another part of the city, but still firmly north of the river, a man is awake, despite the hour. His name is Bonner, William; although total strangers all know him now as Billy, because of the easy intimacy of television. That very evening his face had filled the screens and men in pubs had stopped drinking to nod agreement with each of his pronouncements. The man in the black leather jacket stood for law and order, a phrase he repeated with sinister, yet reassuring, effect. It was another of his customary unsmiling appearances. He took pains not to be filmed or photographed any other way.

He looked at himself in the bedroom mirror. There was a tic under his right eye. Once he had heard it said that if a politician ever sweated on television, he was done for, no matter how good his words sounded. If that were true, where would a quivering nerve land you? He had a bad dream of his own face starting to twitch some night. His appearances were almost always live, seated in a chrome and leather armchair before a glass table with

8

its tumblers of tepid water that no one ever seemed to touch. Around his temples were still traces of make-up. The beige blush marked him out as a celebrity, even if the people didn't recognise him by sight, and come up to shake his hand in the street. But all of that had lost novelty for Billy Bonner. Only if it ceased, was what really mattered to him. His life, it seemed, was spent more and more these days forestalling events instead of initiating them.

He thought of the man who had been executed earlier, a man he had never met, but who, nevertheless, had been despatched by his order. That was a token assassination for the young Turks. He wondered what it must have been like to pull the trigger. His own pistol hung in its shoulder holster over a chair beside the bed, but that had never been fired at anything except paper targets. Now he crossed the room and slipped it from its supple sheath. He fingered it curiously. With the door closed, and the rest of the house sleeping, he could indulge in fantasies. Sometimes he would practise fast draws at his own reflection, varying his posture, standing, lying, crouching, sitting, to suit the scenario. It was delusion, of course. He had too much knowledge of the real thing, when it arrived, to believe it could ever be the way it appeared on any screen. There was nothing neat about it. Bowels loosened, there was whimpering, and the killing occurred in the stink of a car, or beside a hedge, in a muddle of stabbing, kicks and inaccurate shooting. His position now, in the organisation, shielded him from direct involvement in any of that, but he had sufficient memories from his earlier days to tell him that nothing could have changed. When Billy Bonner read in the papers those inquest details, which sickened or secretly excited others, he never allowed emotion to enter his mind, for where that ordinary citizen saw only a half-column of print and thought of someone dying in the time it took to read it, he, Bonner, knew the truth. That terrible hoard of secret knowledge set him apart.

His doctor, who had been treating him for nervous tension, said he must try not to let his mind dwell on things. He could have got that for himself out of any Christmas cracker, he told himself. For that matter, at greater length and expense, from any of the books he would buy at one time. Dale Carnegie had seemed then to be the answer, when all of his first business ventures were going out one by one like candles on a cake. He thought of how green he must have been to trust that smiling, fatherly face on the paper covers. Positive thinking was all very well, but it seemed it needed to be backed up with something more substantial. What he held in his hand, and what it stood for, had supplied that for him. For the time being, he would continue to use what it provided.

In the next room his wife slept soundly, her little amber bottle close by on the bedside table. She moved about the house as if she were swimming underwater, no longer weeping behind locked doors, as she used to, but he had discovered she was reading religious tracts and books which arrived by post. That made him more uneasy, curiously enough. He had found something underlined: *He who lives by the sword* . . .

But, in the mirror, all he saw was a man approaching middle age in a plaid dressing-gown, holding what looked like a toy in his hand. He sat on the edge of the bed. There were so many things best left alone. Brooding was a fruitless pursuit; for the weak, and for women.

At that moment the phone rang and he started. It made a cry like a bird, much worse at this time of night than its predecessor's old-fashioned jangle. He looked at it, shrilling away on the table beside the single bed, knowing he must answer. He thought, Duff has botched it. He has given the wrong message to the newspapers. Earlier, he had sounded drunk, something about Galloway and – pot-shots. Could that have been the word? Duff was his wife's useless brother. Another of the clan, a younger version, snored downstairs on a settee.

Billy Bonner picked up the phone, just as the man at the other end was about to ring off, ready with "Wrong number" before the fool – he thought – could blurt out anything else for the wrong ears. The pips came and went, but another voice spoke, softly, nervously. "Bonner Security?"

"It's outside business hours." A cough. Silence. "Are you on our books Mr —?"

"Account number 2–0–7." Coming in a rush now.

Bonner turned pages quickly, found a reference, spoke into the phone. "Yes, Mr Hill, I see we've done some business in the past. Why don't you call round tomorrow. You know where we are."

"No," said the voice, "I can't – it wouldn't . . ."

And so it began, the halting recital he was used to by now. Reading between the lines, or alternatively, putting the right words into an informant's mouth, because of that unknown

10

presence listening in somewhere across the river, had become a game for Bonner. He usually enjoyed his own performances, more for the frustration they caused the patient, bleary-eyed phone-tappers, than for any intelligence he might manage to elicit. They were also closer, he felt, to what he considered his true vocation to be – namely, a businessman, pure and simple. He saw himself behind a desk wielding power with a hand-set, when all of this had been put at his back.

But the man talked, gaining confidence, and, as he did so, occasionally Bonner wrote on a pad. Then the receiver was replaced and the two were cut off, the sweating ward-orderly in his phone booth in another county, and the man with his words on paper. He looked down at them – a patient's name and case-history, a timetable of his eating, sleeping and medication, other details of a more general nature. They constituted something most important and must be acted upon without delay. Bonner began to pace the room. Once he drew the curtains apart and looked out at the street and the night sky beginning to brighten over the roofs of the housing estate. It seemed to him unfair that, while the rest of the world slept, he had to wrestle with intricacies which drained him and which added little or nothing to his own private ambitions. And he felt as if the turning cage he was in was speeding a fraction faster each day. He walked, he sat, sometimes he stretched himself out on the made-up bed, but eventually a plan had formed and had been tested for flaws. It would do, it would have to, he told himself, for any time spent on elaboration could be dangerous. He looked at the phone, but decided against it.

On the landing he paused to listen. There was the dripping tap in the bathroom, of course, and the cistern's jerking hiss. Most men would have fixed those a long time ago, but such things went without attention in this house. His wife never nagged him either, as other women would, but picked her way uncomplaining among the broken and faltering equipment. At the door of the boys' room he put his head close to the chipped jamb. The younger one was grinding his teeth in his sleep. He was closer to his mother, had begun to moon about the house with that self-same expression of hers. His brother slumbered soundly in the upper bunk bed. A very different story there.

Billy Bonner stood in dressing-gown and slippers at the heart of his sleeping household considering his existence. It was here, all around him, all that mattered to him: family, defenceless in their beds, never more so than at this hour, possessions, and that wad of notes cached away under the tank in the roof-space. He ached with the weight of it all, enough to have to carry without this new and added burden that was borne on a phone call. He went downstairs into the dark sitting-room and punched Young Terry awake.

"A fine bloody bodyguard you're turning out to be," he told him. "Take a message to Galloway, and I don't care what time it is, or where he might be. Tell him I have a job for him. And tell that Scotch bastard to be here first thing. Pronto."

3

NEXT DAY was a Saturday. It dawned fine and warm, temperatures were expected to be well above average for the time of year. The prospects looked perfect for all sports fixtures. But first, the announcer on the eight o'clock news reported on the prelude to what was usually referred to as "the weekend violence". Two bombings, three robberies – all at off-licences – an unidentified middle-aged man found strangled on some waste ground, and an attempted shooting in the suburbs, the victim, a well-known Catholic doctor, now critically ill. Detectives waited by his bedside.

He hadn't heard the news, neither he nor his yawning driver, but when they arrived at Number Eleven, Sperrin Way, it became obvious that the others, waiting for him, had. Duff was there, hung-over, but smirking, while Bonner was finding it difficult to contain himself. He had locked himself in the small, chill dining-room, rarely used. They could hear him moving about, his occasional curses as he bumped against furniture. He was preparing a fresh communiqué for the press, television, the radio, and there was no way in which the words, or their author, could be made to sound any less foolish.

Galloway sat at the kitchen table with the two brothers-in-law. Both were drinking cans of Harp from the fridge. The room was full of cigarette smoke. Duff's face was beginning to flush. He would be drunk again in an hour, and kept asking Young Terry to go out and buy the morning papers. He was the sort who probably kept a scrap-book, thought Galloway. By the time the pubs opened, he would be a hero again.

"In the intensive care unit, that's where they have him."

"So you keep telling me, Duff."

"Maybe it's only a bluff. Maybe you missed him altogether."

"And maybe you're this year's Brain of Britain."

Young Terry laughed. He was the heavyweight of the family, his girth something of an embarrassment to the rest. Instead of inspiring fear, as he would have liked, his proportions merely attracted mockery. He ate, drank and smoked steadily to dull his misery, so, now, remembering, he stopped laughing and pulled the ring on another tin of beer with his teeth.

Mrs Bonner's pale face appeared at the door. "Is Billy ...?" She gestured weakly in the direction of the closed dining-hatch. Her brothers ignored her.

Galloway said, "Give him five more minutes, missus."

"He said he'd run me down to the shops. It's the only chance I have. Everything's gone if you don't get there before twelve, you know."

There were bluish smudges under her eyes, and her hair was clenched in curlers that bunched enormously under a light scarf. Galloway looked at her in much the same way he had appraised the man on the stairs of his house the night before. There were times when he felt certain that some people didn't belong to the same species. In Duff's case, of course, he was sure of it. Mrs Bonner saw him smile at his own private joke, and appeared confused. She gathered her garment about herself and dabbed nervously at her hair. Her hands shook, he noticed.

"There's tea-bags in the tin," she said. Then, "Maybe you'd like a fry?"

The other two sucked reflectively on their chill cans of Harp. Galloway said, "Would you like a cup yourself, Mrs B?" and the beer-drinkers looked at him, startled. The woman seemed even more disturbed, mumbled something, then backed from the kitchen.

The gallantry had risen quite spontaneously. But, on reflection, certainly not out of any feeling for fine manners, nor even pity for the drab being in the quilted housecoat. It was merely something tried out, and on. He enjoyed seeing faces change, grow vulnerable like that, and so contempt for their owners only deepened that much further.

At nine-thirty Bonner emerged from the other room with a folded sheet of blue notepaper in his hand. He didn't speak or even look at them, until he had read over what he had written, mouthing silently. His hands had a tremble too, Galloway remarked. He was wearing a heavy Arran sweater over his pyjamas and was unshaven. He tapped the paper.

"I have to hear about this on the fucking wireless, so I have."

Young Terry choked on his beer. "Billy, sure, I was nowhere near the place." They looked at him with contempt.

"Oliver Hardy," said Bonner. "Aren't you supposed to be out in the hall? On guard?"

The large youth rose with a red face. Puppy-fat hands bunched, then encircled five, not four, of the unopened beer cans on the wet table.

"No," said Bonner. "You've guzzled your quota. We don't want to have to hi-jack another tanker just for you."

Duff guffawed, and even Galloway permitted himself his first wintry smile of the day. It was enough, however, for the small man in the outsize holiday sweater, now pacing the floor. "And *you*, what about *you*?" Galloway continued to roll his cigarette. He knew his hands showed no suspicion of shake.

"He was to be bunged and he wasn't bunged!"

"He was bunged."

"Not for keeps, he wasn't. Not for keeps."

Galloway ran his tongue delicately along the edge of his dark, liquorice-tasting paper, completed the tube, pinched both ends. "Well, you can't win 'em all. Can you?"

Bonner and Duff stared at the perfect black cigarette. Duff said, "How do you do that?" Then Bonner yelled at him to get out and join his brother.

When the door closed, he ran the cold tap violently, and poured himself a glass of water. Billy Bonner neither drank, smoked nor took drugs. It was also rumoured that he exercised daily with a

15

Bullworker in the privacy of his bedroom.

Galloway said quietly, "There's no sense in shouting, you know. Even at him."

"Haven't I every right to? Haven't I?" Galloway merely shrugged. "It's only me who looks the fool."

He broke off to cross to the window above the sink. "How can you breathe the air in here?" He inhaled deeply, hands on his hips.

Galloway recalled an Army P.T. instructor, a much-hated, fanatical, Welsh dwarf, a great one also for flinging windows wide. And cold showers, first thing. One of the lads had sawed the parallel bars through before one of his demonstrations.

"Now, Ned, you know what I think of those two cowboys out there. Not to mention most of the others. None of them in your league. But now, what do you go and do? I'll tell you. You go and let me down, so you do."

Deadpan, Galloway replied, "That quack has got four slugs in him. All at close range. Believe me."

"But what about the news?"

"You shouldn't believe everything you hear on the B.B.C."

There was silence in the kitchen. Outside in the overgrown garden birds sang, and a man beyond the fence whistled just as merrily on this first fine morning of his weekend. Vacuum cleaners were starting up all along the street, and bedcovers coming off. The day ahead was for tinkering with cars, do-it-yourself and the afternoon viewing of Grandstand. In this one house, behind drawn blinds, there was to be none of such things, and, if any of the neighbours found their thoughts straying dangerously in that area, they very quickly occupied themselves with other matters.

"What about this new job? The one that couldn't wait."

But Bonner was still in the mood for raking over last night's ashes. "That bastard had it coming to him. We warned him three times. You know that? He had his chances, let me tell you."

Galloway could see that Bonner desperately wanted him to ask about the man, what he had done to deserve his fate, but he continued to puff in silence. The pale smoke rose and was sucked in an eddy towards the open window. He was never curious, had no desire to know or be told a thing. Someone like Bonner would never be able to understand that; someone like Bonner wanted only to smear him with his own mess.

"They were bringing the wounded men up to him after dark. That bastard was treating them. In his own house." The outrage of it had deepened Bonner's colour. He struck the table repeatedly with the flat of his hand. "Scum like that don't deserve a quick end!"

Galloway looked at him. "What's all the fuss about then?" he said quietly. There was a pause.

"Ned," said Bonner, "let there be no mistake about it, we are fighting a war. Some people don't know it yet, but we know, you and me. Some people have let themselves get lulled into a state of near pig-ignorance. You've met two prize specimens in this house already. As long as the trough is always full – you follow me? Now, God knows, in times like these, we've got to make the best of what we've got, but I think, you and me, we both know we can do better. If we don't, we'll go under. We'll all go under. You may not believe this, Ned, but there have been times when I've said to myself, what's the point of the exercise anyway? Why not give it all back to the Indians? But then I think to myself, isn't that just what they want you to say, Billy boy? Isn't that just what those bastards have been waiting and saying their prayers for? Eh? Doesn't it strike you that way, too? It should, Ned, for, never forget, we have the same ancestors, you and me, the same blood in our veins, because we all come from that same wee spot. Twenty miles of salt water was never any hindrance in the past, and won't be when the time comes round again."

For a moment Galloway wondered if he was going to clasp his hand. It looked very much like it. The thought repelled him. All his life he had heard men talk this way, on platforms or street corners, then in pubs, later in smoky crowded kitchens. Whether to convince themselves or others was something he had never bothered to go into very deeply. He had listened and he had watched. His own father had talked that way, the only subject that ever seemed to set him alight, that made him want then to strike out at things, him and his sisters included, until they learned to stay out of range. They would listen below the window until the noise overhead had died down to a grumble, and then to a heartbroken sobbing. It was the old man. That cut no ice, of course, after a night spent shivering in a black and pissy close. All of it came back to him, those rotten years, the blowhard politics. He hadn't travelled very far, it seemed to him.

"I'm still owed for last night," he said.

17

Bonner's face turned bleak. He rose and went to a tea-caddy on some open shelves. Galloway saw his hand go in, then re-appear, holding a fan of fivers. The notes fell on the table at random, and Bonner watched him as he tidied them into a bundle.

"The rate has gone up," he said. "And will do, every time Duff and Tweed are along. I nearly had to walk home last night."

"How much?"

"Another twenty." The Queen's head fluttered down a further four times.

"You're a cool one," Bonner said.

"It's only money, Billy."

Bonner winced and went over to the window for some more deep breathing. Galloway often wondered just how far he could push these people, but then, experience had taught him that the limit seemed to stretch the more you pressed.

"Tell me something, Ned." Bonner spoke with his back to him. "Tell me something. Is it only the money?"

"Isn't it for us all?" There was silence.

"Dangerous talk, Ned."

"You asked me."

"We don't get many like you, Ned. Some people mightn't understand it. You. Not like me."

"Well, then, it's all right then."

"I hope so, Ned, I sincerely hope so."

They faced one another. Galloway knew he was being scanned for a sign that the message had gone home. He couldn't think of how to look repentant, so he busied himself instead with the makings of his next smoke. Bonner seemed satisfied with a bowed head, at any rate. He was like a pouter pigeon, and so very proud of his lightness of foot, too. Something of a ballroom dancer in his young manhood, Galloway had heard it said. There was very little of that any more. Going in for your bronze was really the thing at one time . . .

Bonner said, "This new job, it's not your usual line of country."

"Oh?"

"No. We want someone picked up, and we want this person handled with care. He'll give you no trouble."

"Someone I know?"

"Not personally. We have photographs, all the gen you'll need. Time, place, opportunity. But – it has to be today."

"*Today?* In daylight?"

"Today. You'll need help."

Galloway considered, with an unlit cigarette between his teeth. He boxed the notes thoughtfully as if putting a price on the undertaking. Agreed, he thought. But with one stipulation.

"I want to pick my own troops. A free hand?"

Bonner looked at him carefully and, after a pause, just as carefully, answered.

"A free hand. Just deliver the goods. And, Ned . . ."

"Yes?"

"C.O.D. . . . In this case."

4

IN THE HEART of that deadest time of day in the wards, after lunch, the rented white van bumped its way almost delicately, over the twin security ramps, through the gates, then on to the driveway leading up to the Cottage Hospital. Riding inside were Galloway, two young Tartans, Tucker Thompson and Jackie Kells, and a girl, Sharon McElwee. The men wore painters' overalls. The girl was dressed in her usual street-uniform of skimpy denim bomber-jacket and wide-legged jeans, brutally sheared below the knee. At first glance she looked like another boy, from bleached crop to the laced, ox-blood Doctor Marten's, but Galloway had decided against putting her into whites along with the rest of them. She would provide that extra ace, her sex and clothes enabling her to move and act independently along the corridors until the time came for her to join forces with them, and hand over the assembled Sterling. In the Transit as they travelled, he had coached her in the mechanics of the weapon. She was a willing pupil; they all were, hanging on his every word.

20

Hero-worship of this order, he had to admit, was distinctly pleasant.

They pulled up beside the flower beds and let the girl down, as if they had merely given her a lift. She walked off without a turn of the head, her airway travel-bag swinging innocently. They watched. She would have to pass a parked Saladin to get to the side door marked on the map they had memorised. The army crew lounged about their armoured vehicle. One of them was black. They saw his teeth flash as he opened his mouth to say something about, then to, the girl. Galloway heard nothing at this distance, but could imagine the Scouse accent.

Young Kells whispered, "What's he saying to her?"

"What do you think?" That was Tucker, old and hard already at seventeen. The girl had something of the same steel. Reports about her on other jobs had reached him. He had anticipated how valuable she would prove if and when some chit of a nurse decided on throwing a fit of hysterics. Curious how much more afraid they always were of their own kind in such a situation. Knowledge like that, and the use of it, reflected Galloway, was the real "intelligence", not the other sort, the messing about with street-maps and timetables, that Bonner and his boy scouts set such store by.

The girl walked past the trio of squaddies as if they weren't there. Their whistling and cries increased. Galloway remembered his own stint in the blotched uniform, the relief if some piece of goods ignored you in the street like that, the feeling of renewed toughness it always gave, of all men together in a man's world. Sucker, he thought.

"Okay," he said quietly. "So, she's at the door. Let's move it."

Tucker let out the clutch and the van crept in a steady sweep over the gravel, past the soldiers who were now staring at them, no longer after those tight young buttocks of a moment ago. Galloway winked and nodded in exaggerated yokel fashion out at them as they went past.

"English bastards," breathed Tucker from the corner of his mouth. Kells giggled. He was sitting low and out of sight in the rear, arms clasped about his thin shanks. He was the junior of the unit, but none the worse for that, a young redhead who would follow his best mate anywhere. Towards Galloway he was respectful to the point of reverence.

Behind the hospital there lay a wide and open space, asphalted

21

and bare, except for a single unattended ambulance. "We'll park over there," Galloway ordered. "See that wooden screen?" – pointing – "There should just be enough room behind it," and there was, their stool-pigeon had done his job right for a change.

Through the back doors of the van they unloaded a folding metal ladder, buckets, brushes and paint cans apiece. They strolled across the yard, one craftsman, his two dutiful apprentices, all in white and ready to start work. Kells said, "I served my time once as a painter." The others looked at him. It was a strange thing to say. Kells went red and Galloway said dryly, "Good. You'd better carry the steps then." They all laughed.

The door they entered led directly to the kitchens. Steam, gleaming aluminium, and sinks piled with a mountain of crockery. Lunch had just finished, after all, and a solitary dishwasher, a woman sitting staring at her feet, didn't even raise her head as they filed past. It was a good omen, for Galloway was relying on everyone they encountered being too busy to pay much attention to three more workers in white. They left the kitchen and, for the first time, that sweet-sick hospital smell reached them. Kells was looking pale, Galloway noted. Some people always feel queasy inside such places. He didn't say anything, however, for it was understood that under no circumstances should any words pass until the job was at an end, his theory being that most people can put a face to a voice and vice-versa. There was no point in making it too easy for somebody with a good memory.

Along the corridors they padded, rubber on rubber, and the idea appealed, that of these three mutes at large in single file, and dressed the way they were. Just as if it was in a film. Galloway's excitement grew as they made their way steadily upwards through the old building. His brain was over-active, yet he felt cold as he followed the plan he held in his mind. They kept to the stairs, lifts were dangerous places for the likes of them. Nurses passed, doctors too, once a visitor much too early and already lost. They ignored his request for directions. He glared after them, his brown paper bag of fruit already beginning to show signs of wear. On the fifth floor Galloway sent Tucker ahead to scout for the girl, while he and Kells pretended professional attention to a stretch of painted wall. Sandpaper was applied when a man pushing a trolley went by. The man looked back at them just before he turned the corner.

Then Tucker returned and now at last they were ready for the climb to the final floor and their objective. Room sixty-seven held what they were after, halfway down on the right, the only locked door in the whole of that long and bare corridor. Up the stairs, hugging the smooth inside wall, himself leading, of course, and now the sweat of the earlier ascent was beginning to chill. He could imagine that bright stripe of emptiness waiting, the uniformed man sitting with his back to the wall outside the private room – the complete floor was given over to paying patients. At the top of the stairs, a last look at the other two. Tucker was grim, Kells smiled back weakly. He'd got his colour back, at any rate.

They turned the corner of the corridor. Kells said, "Oh, Christ!" It was the first wrong thing, but Galloway hardly noticed, his attention was fixed so painfully on the *three* people half-way along the passage. There should have been only two, the girl and the policeman in his chair, but another was there, a coloured doctor in a white coat, leaning in an easy attitude up against the wall. All three were chatting and, momentarily, Galloway felt curious as to what they could have found to talk about so miraculously at that particular point in time. His fascination gripped so, he actually began to walk faster towards the group.

The girl was the first to see them. She moved back. The policeman and the doctor stared at her fumbling with her sling-bag, and Galloway breathed to himself, "Not yet. Not yet." Then the two men saw them too, and their attention swung away from the pale-faced girl.

The young copper with his modern moustache called out, "You're on the wrong floor, boys!" Galloway looked uncompre-hending but kept walking. *Only a few more yards*, he repeated to himself, never taking his eyes off the others, for he felt now he could hypnotise this raw farmer's son. Only if the man moved to rise from his chair would he resort to the cold weapon lying like a surprise in the bottom of his bucket.

The Indian doctor was a handsome fellow, shortish but confident, that was clear from the way he held himself. Galloway felt certain he was the one who had been doing most of the chatting-up a moment earlier. There would be satisfaction surely in making someone like that lose all his darkie dash. Distrust took a deeper turn when he saw the doctor murmur something to the guard, who at last had decided to get to his feet. Galloway felt convinced he could have kept him there, if it hadn't been for that.

With a sigh, he brought the gun out into the open, and the young constable looked down at it with mouth dropping, for it was identical to the one holstered in his own belt. Galloway jerked it once, quickly, a language better understood than any other, and slowly those big red hands climbed into the air. The finer, more sensitive ones of his dusky friend were already aloft. Meanwhile, Sharon – good girl – held now the assembled Sterling in the grip he had demonstrated, and aimed at a point where the copper's flak-jacket ended. No one was going to notice if there was a tremble to that blue-black, pierced barrel. A moment only served to sidestep carefully around the two, then he had the nice, comforting weight of it in his own hands. Tucker took the Walther from him while Kells slipped its twin out of the bobby's webbing. It all seemed so simple, and not a word spoken. Galloway exulted. They were a great team, there was no stopping them.

Their two captives allowed themselves to be manhandled, palms flat and pressing on the wall, legs apart and back, a trick of the British Army's that everyone now knew about from those photographs in the papers. Sharon pushed her hand deep into the constable's side trouser pocket from behind, searching for a key, and he groaned loudly, thinking his nuts were for it. The back of his thick, young neck flamed. Galloway felt no real animosity towards him, now that he was so helpless, and so long as he behaved himself.

Sabu, however, was another matter. If anything had gone wrong, that one would have been to blame. He felt certain of it somehow. He put the cold muzzle under one shiny dark ear as a warning of what to expect, then the girl had the key and was turning it in the lock.

Galloway went in first, with his finger to his lips. The man in the bed made no move or sound but his eyes went straight to the weapon. It wasn't pointed at him, and Galloway hoped the significance of that would escape him. He was a big man, but not as big as he had been led to believe, and his face was the colour of chalk. Whether he could travel seemed doubtful, to say the least, but the orders were clear. Galloway went to the bed and ripped down a hanging wire with a switch at the end of it, just in case he misunderstood their intentions. There were flowers and green and yellow fruit in a bowl, books too. All his orders, thought Galloway, all on the National Health.

So this was the great household name, was it, fame spelled out

24

on a gable wall? It was hard to avoid either the sight or sound of that name in the part of town where Galloway had his movements.

The man in the bed looked at him. He showed no fear, unlike the other two, just seemed too sick, or tired, or both, to care. Which was just what the doctor ordered, thought Galloway wryly, as he went to the door to usher the others in.

Tucker cried out, "Jesus Christ, it's *Silver!*" the moment he saw who the patient was. Galloway knew he couldn't help it, but was angered, nonetheless. Some of his authority, he felt, in an instant, had shifted to this stranger in the striped pyjamas.

Kells was led outside, positioned in the corridor, with his ladder, his bucket and cloth, while inside, face down on the cold lino went the heavy young constable and the Indian. They made a fine contrast. Tucker and the girl began trussing the pair of them, using a coil of flex which also had travelled in the bottom of a bucket.

Galloway watched the big man closely all the while. He had scarcely moved. His hands lay on the bedspread, the rest of him propped up on pillows. A book he had been reading had fallen near the foot of the bed. Using the point of his gun, Galloway idly pushed it sideways until he could make out the photograph of the bearded face on the cover. He lifted the paperback and put it into the side pocket of his own overalls. All this time his eyes had not left the other man's, waiting for a sign, something he could fasten on. Then Galloway went over to the coloured doctor and kicked him twice in quick succession. He was gagged by now with his own tie so he could make no sound. Only his eyes rolled. The whites were pinkish, Galloway noted from his vantage point. This time the man in the bed closed his own for the briefest of moments. It was a sign all right.

Tucker and the girl then started putting the boot in too, the policeman, naturally, taking the brunt of it. Galloway sat on the bed, rolling a smoke, watching, letting them get it out of their system. The girl, he noticed, was particularly vicious, but, then, they always were. When they both had started to pant and sweat more than he felt was good for them, he rose to put an end to it. The girl continued in spite of him, Galloway slapped her face, she fell to the floor, lay looking up at him. Again he had the sensation of having seen it in a movie somewhere. People said he looked like Charles Bronson.

In the second bucket on the floor was a white boiler-suit.

Galloway now bent, picked that up and threw it in a ball at the man on the bed. He looked at it as if he had never seen one before.

Galloway said, "Put it on," for there seemed little or no point in the silent routine any longer. The copper, for a start, had gone bye-byes. He didn't even bother to look at the other one. "We don't want you to catch a chill or anything like that, now, do we . . . Silver?"

The mention of his name (or was it nickname, because of the hair) did the trick. The bedcovers came back and they saw he was only wearing the top half of his pyjamas. The legs looked wasted and white for someone so big, but, then again, not so big as the others had imagined. He'll take the biggest size there is, they had told him; outsize for Silver. But when he had pulled the thing on, Silver looked just like a circus clown, swaying there with his blanched face. The girl dropped to her knees and began rolling up his trouser legs for him. They all looked down at her in surprise.

Galloway spoke harshly. "Time to blow." Tucker and the girl took an elbow each and steered the big man out of the room. Galloway locked the door and, with Kells and his ladder in the forefront, they all started at last on the long slow descent.

By the time they had reached the end of the corridor, however, Silver's breath was catching in his throat and his legs were rubbery. Galloway caught Tucker's eye. He knew what he was thinking. Despite the danger, they would have to risk the lift. All watched the numbers taking their brief illumination, even the sick man. Galloway pressed the button and regretted it immediately. "No – five," he said, naming the floor below, and so they went on and down the stairs, one flight only, but enough to kill this man, thought Galloway. He was getting angry again. Maybe *they* wanted him to croak it, this tottering wreck. Boiler-suit for a shroud. It would make a nice touch. Too nice for the likes of Bonner and Co. No, he would deliver this package still breathing. It was the grim promise he made to himself as they stood finally before the closed doors, waiting for their number to light up.

The dull grey metal doors parted in silence, and a man stood looking out at them, the same orderly who had passed them earlier, wheeling his trolley. Now it took up most of the space inside, dirty dishes piled on all its shelves. Galloway said quickly, "No room. Next car." He smiled warmly. The doors shut.

The man hadn't smiled back. Galloway felt a rush of blood, had to control himself, for he wanted to race up those stairs and haul out the man, erasing the surly and suspicious look with his fists. Then the sweat broke on him at a fresh thought. The lift had been *climbing*. Naturally! Christ, the man was on his way to collect the loaded tray inside room sixty-seven! In his pocket was the key. Should he attend to the man overhead as he had the other two, or should he put his trust in the well-known indifference of the type. The lift doors slid open, Galloway hesitated, then he shooed in his flock. He would take his chances. They sank in silence, Tucker, Kells and the girl every so often peering anxiously and closely at the scarecrow in white. His breath was bad, Galloway noted.

At the bottom, he sent the girl on ahead to make her own way out to the open air. They would, as before, pass through the kitchens – one painter more would hardly attract attention. But when they pushed their way into the steam and cooking odours, they found a crowd of women and girls drinking tea around a long table. All were in high spirits and they raised a shriek when first they sighted them. One called out, "What's wrong with your mate?" drawing all eyes to the tall man.

Galloway said quickly, "He can't stand the smell of paint," and there was a roar of merriment.

"Want a cup of tea, Scotchie?" cried another. Galloway, smiling, shook his head.

They were all big women with bare red arms and white caps. The slyest-looking said, "Hey, Scotchie, give us a keek at what's under your kilt," and they screamed afresh.

But the one who had first spoken said, "That big chap looks awful bad. Maybe one of the nurses could give him something," but Galloway explained that all he needed was fresh air, his stomach was none too good, even at the best of times. He lifted his hand to his lips in a drinking motion, winked knowingly, and all the time kept shepherding his little pack of wolves in their clean boiler-suits towards the exit.

The boldest skivvy yelled a parting shot. "Look at his wee earring, would you, girls?" and the door closed on yet another tide of their mirth.

Once outside, Galloway breathed deeply. The air tasted clean. It wasn't only the big man who needed its benefit, it seemed. His own brow felt damp and the clothes were sticking to his back under his whites. He looked at his watch and found it hard to

27

believe they had alighted from the van only twenty minutes earlier. It wasn't the time or place here among the battered bins to slacken off, but that's what he had a crazy urge to do. Just to suspend everything, to look, listen to his own heartbeat. He felt he had been directing something too intently. Now all he wanted was to take his hands off the controls momentarily to see what would happen. The others had no inkling of what was passing through his mind, no notion how driverless they had, in an instant, become. The boys glanced here and there grimly, the sick man had his eyes closed.

There was a loud clattering over their heads and an army helicopter swam into the light. Its shadow slid across the asphalt. The khaki brute hovered for a moment, then fell away sideways at speed to peer down at the next sector on the map. Tucker spat, but not skilfully enough, and Kells grinned as he wiped his chin. Galloway felt the moment pass when he might have done the outrageous; they began to cross the bare and speckled expanse. Underfoot, it felt warm, much warmer somehow than the first time they had walked over it, softer as well. Like liquorice, thought Galloway.

They came close to the parked ambulance, baking in the heat, and something made him look into the front. Through the glass, he could make out a shape, someone stretched out across the seats, someone with a newspaper covering his face. Blue uniform, big black boots, silver buttons – the driver taking a nap.

Galloway touched Tucker on the shoulder, made a sign for silence and caution, and they came to a halt in the shadow of the vehicle, the big man shored up between his two keepers. They continued to press close as though he might fall in the first unguarded moment. They had acquitted themselves well, better than men twice their age, Galloway told himself. He had been right to enlist them, felt pleased at his own judgement. An urge to clasp them there and then, some sign of his regard for their young courage, came over him, but, angrily, he put it from him. It seemed unhealthy; worst of all, soft.

He took the policeman's pistol from under his loose overalls and moved up along the side of the ambulance until he had reached the driver's door. Gently he pressed the hot handle down. There was hardly a click. He opened the door. He had a close-up view of a pair of soles, almost new, and size ten at the very least by the look of them, for the ambulance man slept with

28

his covered head on the seat furthest away from him. Galloway tapped the boots almost politely, the man grunted and his newspaper twitched. "Okay, okay," he muttered. "Where to?" He was still barely awake.

Galloway said quietly, "Take that paper off your face, and open the back doors, like a good boy."

The driver clawed his *Sun* away. His hot red face had been steaming in the folds of the page three nude, and he came bolt upright against the far door. He stared at the gun, at Galloway, leaning on his elbows on the warm leather. His mouth dropped. There was nothing special about his appearance, just another middle-aged man in a uniform, and now badly frightened.

"Think of the wife and kiddies," said Galloway. "You don't want a medal, now do you, dad?"

"No, no," said the man, less in answer to the question, than to the threat of what he saw in Galloway's fist. He began scrambling over the seat into the body of the ambulance, and, when he heard the sound of the doors being opened, Gallowy slapped the dusty side of the vehicle with his palm. The boys would know what to do. Then he climbed in himself.

There were two low bunk beds at his back covered with neatly folded blankets. They looked inviting and cool in the dimness, with their glimpses of clean linen. No one could accuse him of not taking good care of his charge, he told himself, and the big man didn't need to be told what to do either; he collapsed on to one of the made-up beds with a groan, as if all this had been specially laid on for him and had not been an accident which had merely presented itself.

Galloway saw the joke. There was an even funnier side, for wouldn't Bonner have a seizure if they rolled up to Number Eleven in this buggy with its blue light flashing. Not that they would, of course; it would be dumped, just as the original plan was to dump the white van. Transfer to a waiting car had been arranged at a quiet spot near the City Reservoir, the keys to be left inside the near front bumper. Galloway only hoped such a detail had not been entrusted to that well known music-hall act, Duff and Tweed.

The driver said, "Ah, look, fellas, no shooting, please. I'm a Protestant too. Honest to god."

Galloway looked at his sweating face. He felt nothing for this one. Once you put people in a uniform, they were all bastards to somebody, usually somebody too frightened to cut up rough about it. The thing that puzzled him, though, was how he could have tumbled to them so fast, for even though most people in this godforsaken territory had almost telepathic powers in that direction, no one could be that perceptive – or could they? Then he remembered Tucker's tattoo. On his left thumb was his caste mark, a tiny red hand, a dead give-away. In every sense.

Galloway decided to have a little fun. He said, "You're out of luck this time. We're the I.R.A."

The man's face seemed torn between two expressions, one of genuine fear, the other, a desire to share in the joke, if there was one. "I've a bad heart," he pleaded.

Galloway said, "Convenient, driving this." He waved a hand about the twilit interior.

The driver showed his teeth in what was meant for a smile. And then for the first time, they heard the voice of the man on the bed. "Please," he said. "Please," in a soft weakened murmur, but the reproof in that single word was unmistakable. They all turned to look at him, but his eyes were closed. For the second time that afternoon Galloway felt the threat to his authority. He couldn't explain it, but it was there, nonetheless, in the air, like a smell, invisible, yet apparent to all.

"The picnic's over," he said. "I'll be shooting in a minute. *I'm* in charge. Okay?" The last was for everybody's benefit. Galloway Rules O.K. He could see it on walls already. "Okay?"

On his instructions, the driver took his cream machine out of the yard and swung it around the flower beds past the squatting soldiers, who gave it barely a glance. They were feeding their faces and not likely to remark on, or even notice, one of the painters riding out past them now as passenger in an ambulance. He had taken off his boiler-suit by this time.

The route followed was the one originally planned. First, a drive into the maze of leafy residential avenues which surrounded the hospital, then out to open country away from the Motorway and the blue and white arrows all pointing the other way. Too many fools had had their schemes ruined by a road-block thrown up within minutes across those fast and humming lanes. There was also the nearby prison and its patrols to consider. It was why he was so good at his job – if it was a job – he told himself, his talent for keeping everything in his loaf at the same time. It wasn't a case of being big-headed, it was simple truth, fair dues. His mood was happy now, the sunniest he had been all day. The hedgerows whipped past, fields with black and white cows in them, and farmhouses, every one in its own stand of timber. It looked like a foreign country with the sun shining on it.

Then Tucker, Tucker of little faith, broke the silence. "What about the van?" he asked from the shadowy rear.

"What about it?"

"Well, won't it —"

"Leave the headwork to me," snapped Galloway. "Just you enjoy the ride, sonny boy."

Lack of imagination. If anything, it made him more sad than angry. Then, relenting, he put a hand inside his leather jacket and brought out a bottle. "Pass it around," he said.

He heard giggles from the back. It was only a cheap South African sherry, of the type the winos drink, but it worked fast and was not potent enough to have any real worries about. In the driving-mirror he watched them grab it from one another like kids on a picnic. The man on the bunk was forgotten, as something close to a party atmosphere developed all around him in the dim confines of the travelling vehicle. The girl's voice began to rise at intervals above the deeper tones of the boys, as they pushed and pulled her about. She was trying to excite *him*, Galloway alone, he could tell that by the way her eyes kept darting to him, for the mirror was angled so that he could see everything without being observed.

He rode at the driver's side with his arm resting on the window ledge, at ease with the world. From his little tin box he took out papers and the makings of a smoke, nothing very strong, mainly loose Erinmore. He pinched the ends, lit up, inhaled. Booze was for the birds, he reflected. One in particular, it seemed, because, as he smoked, smiling to himself, he observed how the girl Sharon was gradually putting up less and less resistance to those two terriers, Tucker and Kells. The mirror held the three of them and their panting antics, their young faces, even the girl's, flushed and growing serious by the second.

The smell of the weed, like burning grass, filled the cab and drifted back to the man on the bunk. He had his head turned to the moving bodywork, away from the sights and sounds, and now this strange new scent, even more threatening. Galloway turned, grinning in that instant, to look at him, as if he could read his thoughts. The others didn't seem to notice, or care even.

31

From the pocket of his overalls, which lay in a heap at his feet, Galloway took out the man's book, the one he had been reading in hospital, the one with its author's bearded face on the cover. It was a famous face, no doubt about that. He opened the paperback at random. *The best fighter is also the most political man, and he is more fit than anyone else to become a leader after the war is won,* he read. It had been underlined. He began to leaf through the pages, searching out similar passages. There were enough of them to make the journey pass quickly. He wanted not to miss a single one. It was an undertaking he set himself to complete before they reached the lonely reservoir where their car waited.

5

"WEDNESDAY. Seventh of April. Morning drill and kit inspection have just ended, the men now are free to pursue their own activities until lunchtime. The radio is going full blast – all the other Compounds are tuned to the same station. At least we have that in common. Television comes on in twenty minutes. The addicts are in their favourite chairs already, faces turned to the blank screen. There are also others of us practising on guitars, flutes, even a violin. One man requested a set of drums, but the line has to be drawn somewhere, even though, I understand, he worked outside professionally in a group. He now practises on folded newspapers with wire brushes, all that remains of his kit. Some of the men laugh at him, and I've had to lecture again on the importance of keeping up skills. I don't enjoy this, but we're still an army, even if we are behind wire. Inside Cages like these, self-respect is more important than it is to someone walking free on the streets. If shaving every morning with blunt steel and cold water becomes a means to that end, then that's how we will start the day. When some of the younger volunteers protest about all the spit and the polish, I tell them that while we are in here we are our own worst enemy, and that if we impose our own routines, then it is no longer bull but self-discipline. Only when something is foisted on us from the outside should it be resented. The logic of it escapes some of them. When jankers or a week's fatigues, cleaning the toilets, also fails to drive the point home, then they end up in here, in the Drying Hut, for this is where interrogation and the more serious disciplining is carried out. It's the only place in the Compound where there can be any form of privacy. Up to now our captors haven't realised this, or else they're content to ignore it. The floor is solid concrete after all, so tunnelling would be a waste of time, even for some of our Colditz fanatics. In here among the hanging laundry and the clothes-horses, you can't be disturbed. More to the point – overheard. If someone did decide to go against orders and put an ear to the door, he would certainly think the old man had gone over the top at last. Talking to yourself, after all, is one of the first signs. We've had a few who went like that. A prime pastime in here seems to be spotting the nutter before he spots you –"

One of the men in creaking black leather – all of them around the table were wearing identical new jackets, for some reason – reached forward and punched the stop button. Instantly the laugh on the tape was sliced off, his own laugh, and, great as his humiliation had been, listening to the rest of those recorded confessions, that fragment ringing out, then being so brutally docked like that stung, curiously enough, worst of all.

His mind, he noticed, had started acting in that way, sudden shies away from the realities of where he was, and these seated men so silently watching him. Seconds ago, another instance, the idea, then the image of all five being kitted out at party-rates in some specialist outfitters suddenly swam into his head, and as quickly went. Crazy? The events of the past days and nights seemed now like a conspiracy aimed specifically at driving him that way. He wondered how much longer it would take.

They had certainly spared no expense. He thought of the manpower alone. The one they called Galloway, his trio of giggling recruits, then a succession of "minders", then the one he took to be a doctor, for, despite his shaky hands and rough appearance, he had examined, then injected him. Finally, the five wise men. It was like coming face to face at long last with the inner

34

council after being passed through the grubby paws of a series of flunkeys.

Not that there was anything ritzy about the place he was now in. It reminded him strongly of the sort of depressing room to be found above a bar, little used and, when it was, as functional as a public toilet. The walls were bare except for a whisky distiller's calendar, and an oval mirror hung at an angle over the empty grate. There were chairs of the folding, slatted variety and a table, badly scarred, burned and ringed. On its surface now were further bottles and glasses to add to those patterns. Also sitting there was the cassette machine. It too was tightly encased in shiny black leather, like his interrogators.

The plump one, who had stilled the tape, said, "Do we want to listen to any more?"

"Not necessary," said the man on his right.

"Anyway, we've heard it all."

The last man to speak turned red and shifted on his hard chair when they all looked at him. Younger than the rest, in his middle thirties, at a guess, he exuded aggression and impatience. He was also wearing a toupée, its dyed tint at variance with his much fairer sideburns. Another of the men around the table was also wearing one, the prisoner noticed. He thought of them bald, or going bald, under their expensive hair-pieces – the name the makers preferred to call them these days, he understood. It should have comforted him, as one with no problems of his own in that direction, but it didn't. Instead, there was the creeping sense once more of being in the wrong place at the wrong time. He remembered when it was considered a mark of effeminacy to wear a wig. Had everything stopped for him these past ten years?

Billy Bonner now spoke. He was the only one the prisoner knew – someone from the old days.

Two of the others were faces and names he had seen in the newspapers or on television. The rest were strangers.

"We just wanted your reaction, Silver."

"Reaction?" His own voice when it came sounded rusty, unused. It struck him suddenly he had hardly uttered more than a few words since he had been taken from that hospital bed on the fifth floor.

"That's right. Better still an explanation. We think we're entitled. I mean, don't you, Silver? Don't *you* think now you owe us some sort of –"

"Cut the crap, Bonner!" It was the young angry one. Beads of sweat marked his brow. "You should have been a fucking clergyman, you know that? Not a . . . not a . . .". He faltered.

Bonner regarded him with pity. "Not a what?" he murmured. "Not a what, Sidney?"

One of the other men stirred. "Point of order. No names, no packdrill."

Young Turk muttered, "Point of order. Christ!"

The moment passed but it was obvious now where the real weight of power lay. The other three at the table were slow, secret men. They would never show their hands here, or anywhere else if they could help it. For the moment they were content to wait and to watch. Such knowledge was the smallest of consolations, he reminded himself, but it looked as though from now on he would have to hoard any such trifle the moment it fell his way. If he were to survive. It was a word he was in the habit of using to the men in the Cage. Yet he very much doubted whether cold shaves and showers could help him here, now, or in any future situation held in store for him.

"Have one of these."

Bonner was coming around the table with a full can of beer in his fist. "Nothing stronger, I'm afraid, Silver. Still, I suppose it's been a long time between drinks for you. Eh?" He looked back at the table for approval. No one laughed.

Once upon a time little Billy had been something of a man around town, well within his own class, of course, a familiar figure arriving at the dance halls with his pumps wrapped in brown paper. That's when he had first got to know him as one more of the gang eyeing the talent, chancing his arm with the rest of them. This city had always been a small place. Most people got their nicknames early on. Marge and Gower was what the regulars had dubbed Billy in the Plaza, Orpheus, Maxim's, Caproni's. The dated old names echoed in his head, past haunts, with their smells of perfumed women, orchestrated music, low lights, and he felt afraid that the man watching him, this older, plumper jazzer now reaching him a beer, would read his thoughts and gain further secrets. He drank quickly, then spluttered, as the foam got in his nostrils. This time they all were amused.

His own voice cut above their laughter, but it issued from the black box on the table. The fat man had touched the button again, but for no reason it seemed, this time, other than boredom, or his own clownish whim. He cradled the machine in both hands, staring down into its revolving heart.

The prisoner, with his beer halfway to his lips, heard himself say, "... not easy to master. There's no going back, no changing anything. There's the feeling too, that you must mean everything you say, even though it's only a machine you're talking to. It doesn't offer any help, it just keeps on taking everything down, like something in a courtroom ... That bit should be wiped. Irrelevant. It's got nothing to do with –" His voice stopped.

Bonner said, "But it wasn't, was it? Wiped. It's all there, Silver. Every last word. Or should I say, *here*. Show him."

The fat man – he saw him now as his principal torturer – put his hands into the drawer and pulled out a number of cassettes in their boxes. He arranged them carefully on the table. There were six, seven including the one in the machine. There was no need for him to count.

"Nearly four and a half hours. You see the interest we take in you, Silver. Giving up all that time. And we're busy people." Bonner was still doing the talking, his fingers spread out like someone behind a consultant's desk, and taking his time about getting to the unpleasant part, because he was enjoying himself.

"The thing is, Silver, what to make of all this?" He touched the boxed reels delicately, moving them into ranks. "We're at a bit of a loss, I may as well tell you, comrade. I mean you're still a wee bit on the young side to be dictating your memoirs."

One of the silent ones smiled at that. The prisoner recalled that he had escaped assassination only a month ago, his life spared by the poor marksmanship of the customary two teenage callers at his front door. He had been seen on News at Ten pointing to the bullet-holes in his woodwork. The house he lived in had a rustic slice with *Dunrovin* on it, fastened to the gate. The television picture had faded out on the name.

"None of us had any idea you were such a deep thinker, Silver."

"A real fucking ego-tripper, if you ask me!" It was the young one again.

The prisoner wondered if his rage had not something to do with his hair or, rather, lack of it. A constant reminder was there after all in the fat man at his side. The single bulb overhead shone cruelly down on both their heads. Proof of vanity was there for all to see. For that reason alone, it seemed to the prisoner, they might be the most dangerous. Yet that word still had no real meaning, had it, for whatever the doctor had given him still swam in his veins. It was as though there was a layer of something between any threat and his reaction to it. These men were here, they were talking to him and about him, he was in their hands, yet he couldn't fully grasp the consequences.

Bonner said, "No, I don't think so. That's a bit too simple."

"Amen. Bishop Bonner has spoken," sneered the young one.

Bonner's face went red. "You lot don't go in much for head-work, on your side of the river, do you? Kick and rush."

"We get results, sunshine."

"So did King Kong."

The prisoner wondered why no one laughed.

"Your trouble, Billy, is you're too good for the likes of us. I mean, is it really true you've put your name down for the Open University?" That did raise a laugh, however. In the same instant, the mocked man was on his feet with his coat swinging open. They could see the butt of a pistol – particularly the prisoner from his isolation in the middle of that bare and dusty floor. For a second only, he closed his eyes on the scene. He needed rest badly. All he could think about was the ache in his bones. Gunplay, if it was on the cards, seemed almost irrelevant. He heard the young one cry, "The bastard's packing a rod! He'll have us all lifted!"

"I've got a licence!"

The anger had gone from Bonner's face. Quickly buttoning his coat, he appealed to the others. "It's for my own protection." He looked frail suddenly, almost tearful.

One of the silent ones spoke, "Protection or not, rules is rules. No shooters."

He had a heavy bass voice, the sort of accent too, the city comedians love. In the shipyard areas his might was legendary. The prisoner knew that. To command such a tribe for as long as he had was something of a minor miracle. The prisoner somehow took comfort from that fact, that he was not like the others, these new men with their toupées and identity bracelets and hard, modern manner. They had modelled their image on what they saw on television. It was obvious to him. For the second time his thoughts were veering. His eyes must show it, he told himself. He blinked rapidly, brushing an imaginary speck from his lids.

The man he felt he now could trust leaned forward and addressed him directly. "You might be a big cheese where you've come from, but you aren't there now. Here, *we* rule the turf. Answers is what we want, and answers is what we're going to get."

The others looked at him with admiration. The heavy man sat back. He made a gesture with his right hand; it said, that's how it should be done. "Savvy?" The prisoner couldn't tell whether the last was for him or for the others. It might have been for all of them.

Then they all started in on him. He braced himself, hands fastened to the hard seat of his chair. Pain in his palms might help him through this. He felt a little of his confidence return as he thought of that. It was strange.

"Why did you make the tapes?"

"Have you done a deal with the newspapers?"

"Television?"

"A book?"

"Life-story?"

"Why didn't you pass the word out you were going into hospital?"

"You *have* done a deal, haven't you?"

"Free passage?"

"Toronto?"

"Why are you reading Che Guevara?"

"You're a Red. Aren't you, Silver?"

"Aren't you?"

"*Aren't you?* "

They had run out of questions, and so soon. They looked at one another, surprised at that. Exertion showed plainly in all of their faces. They looked away. While it lasted the prisoner had felt like something hunted; now he knew the relief the prey must experience when the pack has fallen back momentarily, dog-tired. Those hot, burning faces, the hands like paws on the table-top, their whisky breath coming at him in waves – it was like a bad dream again, part of the same one he'd been having ever since his door had burst open on him like that. But it wasn't a nightmare and he wouldn't wake up in the hospital bed, or in his army cot with the others snoring around him either, for that matter. This is no dream, he repeated to himself, no dream. Another phrase asserted itself too. Drugged state, drugged state...

From the room beneath their feet there suddenly arose an odd sound. It broke the silence. He tried to think what it must be, a staccato and metallic ringing, very fast. Then it faltered and ceased. He almost smiled then, realising what it was – a hiccuping fruit-machine hitting its jackpot. The faces before him showed no sign that they had noticed, or even heard. Down there were other men, women too, perhaps, living normally, busy with normal things, drinking, laughing, envying one of their number now scooping up his winnings. It was a world so close, he had only to get through the door, manage the stairs – one flight it seemed to him, as little as that – and walk into that bar. But he had seen too many films. He would reach its safety, then, instead of smiling men in white coats, these new-style actors would appear. The crowd would go quiet, holding their glasses, looking from his face to those of the leatherjackets bunched in the doorway. A girl might laugh out once nervously. It was all re-running in his head. But it was only him who believed in such make-believe. These heavy men certainly didn't, neither did the drinking crowd below. They wouldn't even bother to look up from their own affairs, he told himself. The scripts were different these days. He had been out of circulation far too long. Bonner's look, it said it now. More in sorrow, it seemed, however – like a disappointed teacher's when his prize pupil has been found wanting.

The others were on their feet by now, their attention suddenly elsewhere. They grunted and stretched and talked among themselves. Had they done with him, he wondered, or was this one final ploy? He sat on his hard chair, still the pupil kept after school, while they ignored him, or pretended to.

They had dressed him in a suit many sizes too big for him. He looked like an emigrant, someone who didn't even have to open his mouth to appear ridiculous. A man in his command, a tailor by trade, one of Burton's best, made all his dress uniforms. He made a point of wearing them every time he had been photographed in the Camp. Yes, the prisoner knew enough about such things to understand why they had selected these clothes for him.

He looked at the five men standing around the table. Some were smiling and nodding, lighting cigarettes. It was as though he didn't exist for them, on his dunce's chair. He noted their faces and hands, the skin taut with food and drink, the confidence with which they moved and gestured. Their difference, and the way they gloried in it, made him hate them. It seemed a good sign. He was beginning to fight back, he told himself.

The one he had first thought might be an ally, said to the room, "My motor's here. I'll be off across the Bridge."

"South of the border," sang the young, cocky one, and there was a general laugh.

"Aye, we've all got suntans in Connswater," riposted gravel-voice.

Could he have been wrong about everything, the man in the baggy two-piece had to ask himself, for they looked and sounded now about as sinister as a bowling-club.

"Hasta la vista, Sammy!" and the big, red-faced man went out through the door on a final tide of good-humoured chaff. They all left then, without a backward glance, even Billy Bonner, and their voices could be heard dying on the stair.

The prisoner sat still in the middle of the empty room as silence returned. There was the table facing him, and on it was the tape recorder. He looked at it. Was he meant to approach, put a hand out, then would the door burst open and voices cry out, "Surprise! Surprise!"? He tried to remember if it was his birthday. He shook his head violently as though to shake some sense in or out of it, then lowered it to his palms. If he could only rest, purge this, whatever it was, in some way from his system.

Then the door opened and Bonner backed into the room. He had two glasses of amber spirits in his hands. "Medicinal," he said, reaching one across to the prisoner.

Bonner saw him sniffing. "Three-star. Only the best for a V.I.P. – V.S.O.P." Bonner laughed at that.

They drank and the fiery stuff exploded in his stomach. This time he made sure his face gave nothing away.

"Maybe the doctors warned you off the hard stuff?" asked Bonner.

The prisoner looked at him. It had become something of a resolve now for him not to utter anything. In some strange and superstitious way he believed all his defences would come down in that moment he spoke those first words. They would come out in a croaking rush, he felt certain, outlandish enough to make listeners stop, then put two and two together. He heard himself practising baby sounds in front of a mirror in private somewhere. He shook his head to dislodge the idea and Bonner's glance quickened.

"All right, old hand?" His eyes were bright with opportunity.

The prisoner noted his clothes, really for the first time – apart from the leather jacket. The lilac shirt, the darker-toned tie, the trousers, a muted grey over-check, well-pressed too, and the shoes, with their club heels. Particular as ever about his appearance, was the former champion fox-trotter. That step suited him, the bounce, then rush of it. He had an insane urge to enquire if he still shook a leg, a devastating return to the mundane. At some later stage, for he knew this was merely a preliminary, he might have to pretend that he really was unhinged. Then, well, he might say such things. He drank, keeping attention on his glass.

Bonner said, "You mustn't take it too hard. The lads are rough diamonds."

The prisoner made sure his eyes stayed lowered. Humility flowed from him. Bonner continued swirling his brandy. "Everybody's on a short fuse. You understand?"

A nod seemed acceptable. "But then again, maybe you don't. Can't. Two different words, Silver. Two different worlds." Bonner sighed.

It was a moment when the prisoner could have spoken out. He had the right to be bitter, felt an urge to ask the man sitting on the table showing off his pale socks why he and his friends had never once put in an appearance on visiting days. He let the moment pass.

Bonner said, "No communication, Silver, that's the trouble. No communication. These tapes now," he gestured with his free hand, "well, they could have fallen into the wrong hands, now, couldn't they? Easily. The danger to the cause? Untold, untold. What made you do it?"

It was a relief to realise that he wasn't really looking for answers, at least, not directly. Bonner stroked the side of his nose, while continuing to gaze deep into the tiny whirlpool of Martell still in his glass.

"Interesting, mind you. A lot of soul-searching." A pause. "Ten years, is it, Silver? A man can change a lot in that time. We all have."

He looked directly at the prisoner as though instead of this haggard man in the ill-fitting suit he saw, for a moment, someone from his youthful past, a friendly rival hunting like himself the perimeters of the dance-halls. He laughed. "We haven't had too many intellectuals. Something of a rarity. Though, mind you," leaning forward confidentially, "we could be doing with a few. Just to right the balance. The other side seem to be well supplied in that department. No shortage of failed priests there."

The prisoner registered the jibe. It was rare to hear any mention of religion, no matter how oblique, these days. People were wary, had learnt the lesson well. The world-wide accusation of bigotry had stung like no other.

"All these writers you're keen on. New to me. Except, of course, our friend from Cuba. Power from the barrel of a gun, eh?"

Wrong on two counts, thought the prisoner.

Bonner drank then, a final draining. There was to be no further sociability, for he became brisk and businesslike, jumping down off the table. His built-up heels rattled loudly on the pitted floorboards.

He laughed at the expression on the other's face. "Cheer up, Silver. You look like a wake. Your own."

The prisoner showed his teeth. It was almost more than he could manage. Then Bonner clapped him on the shoulder.

"Time for a little treat," he said. "Something you haven't had for a very long time, old son." He held the door open, still laughing.

6

THE PHONE CALL, when it came, was brief and required no answer. The expected voice simply said, "Three-thirty. Brotherly love," and she was left listening to the purring tone.

She put down the cream receiver and looked at it. No other colour would have been right for this room, she decided. There were times, indeed, when she liked to pretend she was some smart young dentist's receptionist. She would file her nails then, and allow her gaze to take in the muted colour scheme, beige ripening to sandalwood, the two low couches, the glass table covered with magazines.

That's where the resemblance ended, of course. On the floors above, the reading material strewn about for the clientele was much cruder, acts with animals seemed to be the favoured thing at the moment, but even here, where the Tijuana Brass pumped softly day and night, it was difficult to avoid the sight of straining flesh. It glistened from the magazine covers under the lighting like raw meat, pink, but occasionally glossy black. The look on the

44

customers' faces as they browsed among the pin-ups was much the same, it seemed to her, as that she'd seen outside any well-lit display of cuts, joints and carcases. Why were people always drawn to stand gazing into butchers' shop-windows anyway – and jewellers?

She smiled to herself. This job was a lonely one, you never had anyone to share a joke with. Still, it was better, she reflected, than being upstairs, no matter how much money the girls in the cubicles above managed to show for their exertions. And, no doubt about it, Terri, Olive, Trish, Geraldine, Mandy and big Paula certainly earned their "bread". That's what they called it, for they were all English and experienced – except Geraldine, with the freckles.

At that moment the phone rang a second time. She looked at it, thinking of the previous caller. It might be the same voice. She would have to answer.

But it wasn't; the preliminary nervous cough, followed by silence, told her differently. She spoke more briskly than usual. "I'm afraid Miss Terri is fully booked this afternoon. The other staff as well. So sorry," and put the receiver down.

Immediately she felt bad about it, not so much for the lie – all the girls were waiting idly by for the famous visitor to arrive, whoever he might be – but, because she knew the harmless old thing on the other end of the line, and this was the first time she'd ever had to disappoint him. They all suspected he was quite a well-known medical man, for some reason, a specialist of some kind. Young Terri laughed about him to the rest of them. She called him her Marcus Welby M.D. Only the ones the girls liked were ever honoured by a nickname. All the rest were just faces, or that other famous part of their anatomy. As Paula once crudely put it, "Once you've seen one dick, you've seen the lot."

It was funny, she reflected, how so many of them had started off in nursing. She had as well. She looked down at her manicured hands, nails the colour of dried blood – well, not really. Mocha, it said, on the tiny pyramid-shaped bottle on the table before her, and she thought of the times she had plunged them in and out of water, slops and worse, in the wards. She glanced at her watch then, nervous suddenly, lifted the pale phone and dialled. The woman's stuck-up voice said. "At the third stroke, it will be three twenty-five, precisely . . ." There was nothing to do but wait, she told herself. Just like the others upstairs. She thought of them puffing away – all had a heavy habit – then, if their light was to go on, how they would leap up to fan the cigarette fumes away and gargle with the mouthwash. More and more customers seemed to be non-smokers these days.

In the far corner of the room there stood a trolley covered with bottles. That habit, at least, had not declined. She decided she would help herself to a stiff vodka. Why not? All this waiting about was beginning to weigh on her. She poured out the clear relaxing stuff, then tonic, and took a deep swallow. Ice would have been a blessing, but there was little or no time for that. She drained the glass and set it back in its place.

Seated in her welcoming position – the first thing the clients saw was her in her raw-silk blouse, three buttons undone – she blotted her lipstick carefully with a pink tissue and allowed it to drop into the waste-paper basket. She yawned. It was at times like these that she wondered what she was doing in a place such as this. What's a nice girl. . ? No. All that pummelling upstairs, all the groaning and the shouting out sometimes too, it had nothing to do with her. That's how she saw it. She said it to herself. *That's how I see it.* She only saw them before and after; what went on in between was their business, none of hers. She wasn't even curious any more. But the expression on their faces, when they came back down again, still had the power to intrigue. Who would have thought so few of them would look satisfied or relaxed? Most seemed ashamed – she went out of her way to be chatty then; some were hard-faced or brooding, and quite a number tried to get off with her, which seemed oddest of all. She could see it in their eyes, how they would love to have her there and then on the leather couch without any of the upstairs preliminaries. All her skills had to be brought into play then. She would laugh a lot, moving about the room, pretending to be busy, tidying and rearranging the magazines in preparation for the next caller, due at any minute, she would suggest. At the same time she had to be careful not to appear too playful. But they usually went quietly enough, slipping out into the streets and back to their offices or their wives or girl-friends. So far there had never been any trouble that she couldn't handle herself. On reflection, theirs must be the only establishment she knew of that didn't have a man discreetly, but permanently, about the place.

And at that point she heard a sound at her back, which momentarily threw her into confusion. A stretch of heavy curtain hung there. It matched the colour of the wall perfectly, and behind it was a hidden door, and beyond the door someone had just knocked, quietly, but insistently. She looked at the drop of beige fabric, then at the door on the other side of the room, for she had expected her caller to come from that direction, and to ring. The knocking came a second time, and whoever it was seemed unhurried, certain about being admitted.

She went to the curtain, drew it aside, turned the key, and in from the alley-way stepped a grinning Billy Bonner. He said nothing to her, but placed his executive case on the table, then went across to the trolley, where he slowly sank and began examining the labels on the bottles.

"No brandy, Nan? Where's the brandy? I've been drinking brandy."

She shook her head. "Brandy? Brandy?" The words seemed foreign. "There should be some there somewhere. At the back." She leaned over him and he sniffed appreciatively.

"French perfume that rocks the room."

"That dates you, Billy," she said. He laughed. She had never seen him in such good humour. He seemed to gleam. Everything about him, his skin, his leather jacket, buckled Bally shoes, shone in the light. A ring on his last but one finger gave off a matching glint. Then he saw her looking at his case.

"I know it isn't pay-day. You've still time to get the books in order."

He was grinning broadly – he had found a bottle and a balloon glass – and she wanted to kick him where it hurt most, for she had never ever fiddled the ledger, not once, hard as it was to believe.

"Have a drink with me, Nan. I don't like drinking on my own."

"Look," she said, "you tell me whenever you want to close shop. I'll send the girls home. It's only money."

He sighed deeply. She could tell he'd had a few, and prepared herself for what had to follow.

"It's always business with you. Now, why is that? Nan?"

He was edging closer, his eyes sliding over her. The small types are always the worst, she thought. She knew why, of course, but still asked herself the eternal question.

Billy Bonner balanced on the edge of the table and looked down at her hungrily. "Nan?"

She stared back. "Yes, Billy dear, what is it?"

A tiny nerve fluttered suddenly under his right eye. She

47

watched it, fascinated. He swallowed. "I like you, Nan," and then he paused. Then, "We could make music together."

She should have known his reaction, but she had to laugh, she couldn't help herself, the line was so corny, reminding her of the back rows of countless cinemas and every cheap-skate Romeo she'd ever had to put up with. "Oh, Billy, Billy . . ."

His face seemed to snap shut like a lid. She couldn't keep her own eyes off that twitch he had, either. It beat now with greater rapidity. His brandy breath blew on her, and for a moment she knew a fear. All his masculinity was in the odour. Perhaps she did take risks. She knew what they said about women like her, who gloried too much in the power of their own sex. She tried to make a joke of it, put out a playful hand then to pat him on the knee.

He pulled back sharply and, with venom in his voice, "I could pay for you, but I won't. I never have."

"Lucky you," she countered. No thought was in it, only instinct. It made him harder, resolved on retribution. She saw it in his eyes.

"Listen, *cow*," and his fingers closed on her throat before she could move. His face loomed. "You forget who you are. Who owns this kip. Who owns *you*. Don't!"

He released her suddenly and she fell back choking. Her first thought was that he had marked her. Billy Bonner laughed with pleasure when he saw how she fumbled for her mirror. She put it to her face for a moment, then, spending all her fury, hurled it at his grinning mug. The compact missed him by a good yard, struck the wall and fell feebly to the carpet.

"Seven years bad luck, Nan." He sauntered across and touched the hinged disc with his toe. "Yes, seven years bad luck."

Then he kicked it, and fragments of silvered glass sprayed the further wall. He hurled his own empty glass after it. In a matter of seconds he had broken half a dozen others in similar fashion, enjoying himself hugely.

The destruction and the sound of Bonner's laughter was the worst thing to have happened so far. She knew she could never be at ease in this room ever again, his presence like a stain or a foul smell which could never be eradicated. It was as if a burglary had taken place on this, the quietest day of her week.

Billy Bonner watched with the same grin on his face while she piled together her few belongings on the table-top. They looked pathetic. A hairbrush and a comb, her own mug with its zodiac sign, a couple of paperbacks, make-up, scarf, a pen, letters, a small furry toy, its snout ink-stained. She started dropping them one by one into a carrier bag.

Bonner said, "A funny time to start spring-cleaning."

She didn't bother to look up. Why was she taking that silly bear, for god's sake? The drunk who had given it to her had meant nothing to her.

"Or maybe you think you're going somewhere. Is that it?"

"Full marks out of ten."

Some of her courage was returning. In a moment she would be able to look him in the face, she would rise slowly, then she would walk out through the door. To breathe fresh air seemed the most precious of luxuries.

Bonner said, "Before you go – that's if you're really set on it – you'll do us one small favour."

It wasn't a question. He smiled at her, and the nervous pulse below his eyes had quietened. *Us*, she noted. She continued filling the creased Marks and Spencer's bag. The accumulation of a year and six months. It seemed a curious record somehow.

"Nan? Hen?"

She looked at him. How could she have ever been frightened of this pocket edition of manhood, this sorry little fashion-plate, this budgie. Such a list could scald if she only took the notion to let fly. But, instead, she said, "No. You do me a favour."

He smiled back at her.

"Why don't you push off and do your James Cagney imitations somewhere else? Your act stinks. Star Quality, strictly nought out of ten."

"But, how about this for Content, eh?" and he unbuttoned his jacket, and she saw the holstered gun high under his left armpit.

"You mean it's *real*?" she said. She could always come back fast. It was one of her abilities, even at a time like this.

"Oh, it's real all right," Bonner replied, his voice soft and restrained. "You can even have a demonstration, if you like."

He drew the thing out, and pointed it at the picture of women bathing on the furthest wall. "No charge."

She heard a click and her nerve broke. "*Don't, don't!*"

He looked at her curiously, as though seeing her for the first time. "I knew you were like all the rest," he said. "Like every other stupid cow who pushes her luck."

He laid the flat, cold barrel of the gun against her cheek. She

49

tried to pull away, but he held her fast. The metal seemed to burn, there was a smell too. It reminded her of men in greasy overalls.

"You still think this was made in Hong Kong, eh?"

The pressure on her face increased, forcing her to cry out, "No, no, Billy!"

"Good girl," he said and began stroking her other cheek with his free hand. He sighed. "You know something, people like you need an awful lot of convincing. What do we have to do? What does it take before the penny drops?" He cocked his head to one side, as if he expected to hear something. "People like you. Punters. You have no respect. No respect, I tell you. What does it take?"

The two of them sat together in that tastefully decorated room, marred only by the heap of broken glass on the carpet, their faces mere inches apart. There was no sound. The blood which had roared in her head was beginning to subside. She waited patiently for him to release her, like some dumb, defenceless thing. He seemed to appreciate that, for he gave her cheek one final pat, then he went across, and pulled forward the only other chair in the room. He buttoned his jacket, sat down and picked a piece of fluff from his sleeve between finger and thumb. The invisible mote blew away.

"You took a call," he said. "To get ready for a . . . visitor?" She nodded. "Good, good."

Her assent had been unthinking. The memory of those words on the phone and indeed, the earlier message at her flat, the night before – a different voice then, but the same brevity – had all been swept away. Now she tried to concentrate. Billy Bonner looked at her from his low chair. His hands lay in his lap, his legs were crossed, he looked like a man with wares to sell. She wondered suddenly what he carried in his case. It sat on the table, bright hasp and handle facing her. Were there initials? It would not have surprised her.

He said, "There's someone waiting outside, someone we want you to look after. Special treatment, you understand? I'll leave that side of it up to you."

She said, "All the girls are free. Does he have any . . . tastes?"

Bonner laughed. "I don't think he'll be hard to please."

"Okay, then I'll just let Mandy know."

She moved towards the bank of buzzers – one ring to prepare for a client, two to hurry him out, three to call it a day, four for fire, a bomb, the army, police or any other unlikely contingency. Billy Bonner saw to it she never had to count beyond three. She wondered suddenly what would happen if she made a mistake – on purpose. How would our cocky friend here handle all those screaming half-clad girls coming down the stairs in a rush? Even at a time like this she could still appreciate an element of farce in things. It was to be of little consolation however, for she felt his hand on her arm and he said, "Not Mandy, sweetheart. *You.*"

She looked at him. "But I don't . . . I never –"

"I said it was a favour. Remember?"

There was silence in the room. Sounds from outside rarely reached her here. It was a residential area, the avenue outside was poplar-lined and the neighbours led the quietest of lives. Dogs were walked or rose bushes seasonally pruned. There didn't seem to be any children. If the old people behind their curtains ever wondered about the goings on at number fifty-four, no sign of it reached them. The thought of all those bent heads over their needlework made her feel even more defenceless. Bonner's eyes too seemed to say to her to be sensible, to accept her fate. The word made her think of another phrase. Worse than –? But here in this city, there were even things beyond that. She touched her face involuntarily, thinking of blades cutting and stabbing, the precise details to be read in newspapers, photographs that made the worst rumours come true.

Bonner said, "I don't trust those other cows. Not with somebody like our friend outside," but she knew that was only part of the truth. He meant to humiliate her, it was plain by the grin on his face. She wondered what the man would be like. Others who had been "special" too had arrived by the door in the entry, after dark, flushed in the face with food and drink. She recalled one who hadn't been like that at all, dark-skinned, Libyan by nationality, she understood; but, for the most part, they liked their steaks, their brandy and cigars. There had been a lot of Scots on occasions, more interested, it seemed to her, in toasting Rangers than any of the girls, some Dutch and once five fat Belgians. One of them, according to Olive, had a swastika tattooed on his tenderest part. It became a standing joke, to coin a phrase.

Bonner said, to rub it in, "You're really quite privileged – if you only but knew it."

She looked at him. He sighed, slapped his dapper thigh. "I'll bring our friend in then. Introduce the two of you."

She wondered what he was waiting for, why he was scanning her face. She wanted now for him to go on talking, sitting there with his eyes on her so that she could coax from him a secret motive.

He started to rise, his mood changed. He had scented something. "Well, both of you have a ball then."

Crossing to the curtain, he wrenched it aside with slightly more force than was necessary. The door closed and she was alone in the room, staring at the smart black case on the table. She had been right, there were initials after all. W.A.B., she read idly, and wondered what the middle letter stood for. Animal? It made her feel a little better. She moved across to the trolley and quickly poured some Smirnoff into a glass. She was drinking it as it came and grimacing at the taste – god knows what they must have thought of her expression – when the curtain swung and Bonner brought the stranger into the room.

"Nan, meet –"

"Silver!" she exclaimed, in spite of herself. "Silver Steele!"

Later, remembering their first meeting, she was also to recall her first reaction at the sight of that hollow-cheeked and grey figure. They mean to kill him, she thought. And then: am I to be part of it – as well?

7

He lay on his face listening to the piped medley flowing from a speaker high up on one wall. "You Do Something To Me", "That Old Black Magic", "Bewitched ..."

The girl – woman, rather, she was no longer that – meanwhile, was pressing rhythmically down on the small of his back. She didn't seem very skilled. So far, barely a word had passed between them. Gestures, yes, and looks, but little else. It didn't seem strange. He allowed her to knead him while he listened to the evergreens, each tune running painlessly into the next. Everywhere he had been so far there had been music. In his drifting state, the thought, then the certainty of it loomed suddenly like an object out of fog. Even in that upper room, the beat from the bar below had throbbed without pause. All the cars he had travelled in had their radios turned on. One of the boys in the ambulance had a transistor tethered to his wrist. Whatever they had given him (you could get enough on the head of a pin, so he had heard, to hallucinate a roomful) might make him imagine connections, or even a conspiracy, where none existed, but the music was there and had been all along. It was playing in his ears at this moment. "You're Driving Me Crazy", "You Go To My Head . . ." The titles came to him with alacrity after only the first few bars – one of many useless talents. There were quiz programmes where he had beaten the panel to the punch every time, from an armchair. Now he was at it again, old habits being what they were. Another number began – "I Didn't Know What Time It Was" – not an easy one, and sweat began to break out on him suddenly under those stern governess's hands. Only when he stiffened did she desist.

She asked, "Did I hurt you?" and it seemed a strange question to come from someone in her profession. He lay motionless, and after a moment, she resumed the joyless friction. At the time he remembered thinking, do they really pay good money for this? But that was momentary and almost irrelevant, for his mind was gripped now by this latest implication, as sinister as a rat in a drain. He closed his eyes more tightly, when what he really craved was to shut out the music and its sick message. It seemed to be rising in pitch. Already he heard a rodent squeal.

A tune ended on a long trumpet note, then, as if to mock him afresh, the tape started on its loop, after a brief hiccup. "I Hear Music . . ."

"Turn it off!"

He lay in his own sweat and trembled until she went across to the wall. He heard her sigh, stretching, for her build was comfortable. The music fluttered and died and he could hear his own breathing again, as if he'd been in a race.

"You're all tensed up," she murmured. Her hands, for the first time, felt sympathetic. He heard a seagull scream in flight outside the window. Like her voice, it seemed to bring back normality, the normality of streets and people's voices and his own place, as it used to be, in that scheme of things.

"That's more like it. Our business – your pleasure. Your friend Billy invented that one. Remind me to give you one of our cards before you go." More sick jokes, he thought.

He tried to work out what time of day it must be – there was still light beyond the boudoir net of the curtains – and what they would be doing back in that other life he'd been taken from. It was something of a shock to realise that it was there he felt he truly belonged, and not on this speeded-up escalator where forces bunched bewilderingly from hour to hour. He ached now for the old routines, those same restraints which at times had driven others around him to the state he himself was now in. He remembered a man whose crack-up had been signalled by his wanting to go out before reveille each morning to feed the sheep in the fields. Of course there were no sheep – nor pastures, for that matter; they existed only in his head. Once an obsession took hold, it had to grow within. He thought of tubers inching in the dark of cellars or under stairs, roots finally bursting through walls. Once begun, there was no stopping it. He had started sweating again.

He said to the woman, "The music. Is it always the same?" He hoped his voice was under control. "I mean, do they ever change the tape?"

She halted for a moment. "You know, I couldn't really tell you. Do you know that? I mean, it's everywhere these days, isn't it?"

He tried to detect a deeper meaning. There might have been one but it could only be confirmed by her eyes and they were hidden from him. He tried to remember their colour. They might be brown or blue or green... It was a weak joke, but none the less a joke. His mouth had twisted briefly in the damp towel. Then she said, "Turn over," and he did as he was told, twisting, with a grunt. It was surprising how clumsy this whole business made one feel. All the literature, the films, the mythology, lied strenuously, there was no doubt about it.

He said, "I suppose this is what they call a massage parlour..." Her eyes were more grey than anything.

She poured out a generous blob of lotion into her cupped left palm. Baby Oil, he read on the label. "Where have *you* been?" Then her face changed. "Oh Christ, I didn't mean that. Really I didn't..."

"It's okay," he said. "No need to apologise."

For one unguarded moment he felt like throwing himself on her mercy. She looked sympathetic, the sort he would have been drawn to in the old days. Brunettes, on her scale, had always attracted him. More important, of course, was the fact that she was the first person since this nightmare began who had showed any small sign of humanity towards him.

"What's your name?" he asked.

"Nan."

Her glistening palms transferred their coating of oil to his chest

55

and stomach. He wondered how he could get it off afterwards. But, just as he repressed his earlier impulse, he held back on that query as well. Could he seriously believe that she wasn't party to the plot against him? If she were uninvolved, then what was she doing here? What was *he* doing here? All these people and their lives touching him. The list was growing hourly. He tried to put them – *it* – out of his mind. Something malignant in the dark spreading silently, without let-up ... He shivered. How long would it take to get what they had dosed him with out of his system? He closed his eyes. It was pretence, for there was nothing soothing in this damp slapping. This was for men of weight, pashas whose excess wobbled. They would enjoy all this pat-a-cake, he told himself. Some of those earlier, the fleshier godfathers in the upper room, they probably indulged themselves here on this very table. It made him despise them. For a brief moment he day-dreamed about having them for his own bidding back in the Compound. It wasn't quite beyond the bounds of possibility ... or was it? The men he had left behind there dreamed of this, he told himself. The real thing, better than any girlie gatefold. A pity to have to disappoint them ...

Nan was wiping her fingers with a wad of tissues. The look on her face, as she did so, seemed to be one of distaste. Again he had the feeling that she must be new to this game. She wasn't a slip of a thing either, or green. In her early thirties, he would have guessed. She didn't fit, somehow, with her appearance. Her clothes were certainly wrong, but perhaps they didn't all wear hot-pants. She began to unbutton her blouse. He looked up at her, startled by this sudden translation of his thought into her action.

"You can have it topless," but she wasn't asking him, he noticed. Her fingers moved down her front, nails a match in colour of the thin material, real movie-star's nails, glistening ovals, blood-red. He thought of those women who serve behind perfume and make-up counters in the larger stores, mature, heavily-scented, and dressed just as she was. He had finally placed her. The blouse swung open and a fine rounded midriff was exposed. She undid her cuffs and then, with a swift movement, she was standing over him, bare from the waist up. It hadn't struck him that she wouldn't be wearing anything underneath. Any woman who went about like that must be proud of her shape and, as he held his eyes on those heavy but firm orbs, he

56

decided that Nan had every right to be. He felt desire flicker momentarily, but that too had been diminished and damped down along with everything else. He was like someone who could only observe his feelings at a remove, as though glass.

"What's the problem, big boy? Billy Bonner's footing the bill, or didn't you know that?"

"No problem," he murmured weakly back. "No problem."

She was angry for some reason, but not at him, he decided. At herself, or someone else, was closer to the truth of it.

"Don't you like what you see?"

"Very much," he replied.

She looked down at him, and again he had a desire to enlist her aid, but it passed as before. Hands on her hips, she asked, "Do you want a drink? I do."

"No."

"You're a funny . . ." What word was she looking for? He could understand her being at a loss, surveying such a scarecrow. Hospital should have fattened him, but hadn't. The flesh instead had melted from him, as though into the mattress. No one but he, it seemed, noticed anything unnatural about the constant hothouse heat of that place. It was his first experience of the outlandish way things seemed to be conducted on the outside. His system had been at risk ever since.

"Where do they keep the bloody stuff?"

He lay watching. She was absorbed in her search, and he thought of another time, another place, when he might have been able to show his full appreciation of all that firmness and its unselfconscious display. No one would believe him, if the truth of this were ever to be told.

"Sure you won't join me?" She had found a bottle of gin and glasses, and had already poured some. Neat, he noticed. It was hard to tell if a woman had been boozing or not. They seemed to be able to cover it up until they fell down or started weeping. Ten years without their company, yet he still remembered that much.

"How long has it been?" she asked, and this time he felt not so much startled as amused.

"Too long."

"But it's all behind you now, isn't it? You should be celebrating, big boy, not me. Shouldn't you?" and she raised her glass. He liked her calling him big boy.

She was sitting quite close to his bare feet. She seemed more

57

relaxed with a drink in her hand, he noticed. But again that, for him, only added to the sense of unreality he already felt, for it was such details, the charged tumbler, already with its lipstick trace, the jewellery against her bare skin, rings, a neck chain and medallion; most bizarre of all, for some reason, the heavy man's watch she wore. That chronometer, as the small ads were grandly given to describing them, with its black face and luminous characters, so out of place on such a fine wrist, struck him as almost as unreal as the idea of him being at liberty.

"You're in all the papers," she said, sipping her mother's ruin. "Did you know that?" He moved his head to signify that he didn't, hadn't seen any newspapers. "Television too. One thing. Nobody'll recognise you from the picture they're putting out. You haven't been on hunger-strike, by any chance, have you?" She eyed his rib-cage dispassionately.

"I've been sick," he told her. "Nothing but liquids."

She raised her glass. "Join the club," and they both laughed. It was a good moment, one to be cherished, for he didn't know when the next one might present itself. He felt curious suddenly about something. "How did you know who I was? When you saw me, I mean."

"Oh," she said, "I've always followed your career with interest. You used to knock around with someone from the bottom of our street."

"A girl?"

"A girl."

He felt a sudden onrush of sentiment, tears even, for no reason, it seemed, other than that he was at a perilously low ebb. Soon he must release all this self-pity that was mounting in him. He prayed that when he would have his good cry, he would manage to be on his own, the way such things were arranged back in the place he had come from.

Nan was watching him closely. She said, "I haven't even told you her name yet," but her tone was soft. He pretended to be interested. "Dolores Herron. Remember her?"

"Sure," he lied. "Dolores." It made his emotion of a moment ago doubly ironic.

"She wore her hair in a fringe. Lovely eyes. We all thought she was stuck-up, though."

He still couldn't recall any girl. His memory, anyway, wasn't like that. Only specific areas ever lighted up for him, and then, for the barest of bright seconds, at the prompting of a voice, a smell or, on occasions, music. The word stung and he was back once more with his earlier suspicions. The idea of microphones and spy-holes seized hold a second time. He felt like something on a glass slide, being pored over, while this woman softened him up with talk of a past he had never known. How could he have been so bloody green?

He made a move to turn over on the padded board, away from the eyes in the ceiling – a pin-hole was sufficient for their purposes – but Nan's strong hands held him. She resumed a slow and much deeper massage, while her voice rolled on. "All the girls fancied you in your soldier's uniform. We used to watch out for you getting off the bus with your box of chocolates. It was always the Forum you took her to, wasn't it?"

Her spread fingers were moving steadily down to where the towel covered him, and he watched, unable to stop them. "I heard she emigrated. Did you hear that? The whole family. There was one of the brothers came out a doctor. Gerry. Funny the things you remember, isn't it – *big boy*!"

He was naked suddenly. She had his towel bunched in her hand; she held it aloft like a prize. He felt cold where it had been.

"Not so big after all," she murmured, and this time, he could hear the drink talking. "Poor little thing. Let me bring it to life?"

She seemed to sway, cutting off the light. He sat up suddenly, drawing his knees close to his chest, and the pain in his head flared like some bright and cutting lance. Amazement at its ferocity was the thing that gripped him, not its cause, nor even what it might portend. The pain. His brow felt clammy. "You're pissed," he said.

"Why not? If you weren't such a bollocks, you would be too. I thought that's what all you lot wanted, the minute you got out, anyway. As well as the other. What makes *you* so bloody different?"

Again he recognised there was some other target for her anger. She sat down on the couch beside him, as though she had forgotten him already.

"What a shit-house!" Then she laughed. "If Miss Dunn could hear me now." She turned to him. "You remember Miss Dunn's? In Royal Avenue? Secretarial College for Young Ladies?" He had to smile. "So, it is alive, after all. You had me worried."

The pain was going. It seemed to have shrunk to about the size of a coin. He could cope with that dimension, he told himself.

"Forty words a minute. Shorthand *and* typing. The quick brown fox jumped over the lazy hen . . . Ach, maybe I am drunk."

"Look," he said, "I didn't mean it."

She looked at him. "You know something, you're not a bit what I expected." Her elbow nudged his bare leg. "I have you interested, haven't I?" He smelt the gin on her breath, not unpleasant. He had forgotten how perfumed it could be. A desire to reach out towards all that warm, womanly flesh, there for the taking, momentarily tempted him. He remembered those images of lust pinned inside every olive-green locker door. Only later would he realise, then regret, what he had missed.

"Men's legs," she said, matching her caress to the words. "I suppose your trousers rub all those bare patches. They could do with a fortnight in the sun. Like to take anyone with you, big boy? Think about it."

He did think about it, the two of them together on some beach. She would look tremendous, tanned in a white swimsuit. It was true, perhaps he had been away too long, preferring the fantasy to the real thing. What was it – you meet a nicer class of person . . .?

"Copacabana," she said.

"Biggs," he riposted. "Ronald Biggs."

"But *he* robbed a *train*, don't forget." She glanced at him – slyly, he thought. "Yours is owing to you. Gathering interest," then, quickly, "Anyway, what's a few grand to your friend downstairs?" She giggled. "Billy Bonner in Brazil. Sounds like a song title, doesn't it?"

"Where The Nuts Come From." A real oldie. It had slipped out.

"Yes," she said slowly. "Nuts is the word, all right . . . Tell me if I'm wrong, big boy, but wasn't this a nice wee place to live in, once upon a time?"

He recognised the swift change of mood brought about by too much drink. Her voice now hovered on the edge of tears. She was still stroking his skin, but not professionally any more. He hardened himself against this tipsy half-clad woman, for he felt dependent all over again on the whim of others. As it had been all along, he reminded himself bitterly. Taking a chance – but it was now or never – he asked, "Isn't it a bit dangerous to be here with me?"

"Giving succour, you mean? I read that in the papers."

"I haven't seen any."

"You should. You've made the headlines. Three days in a row."

"That's what I meant by dangerous."

"Look," she said bitterly, "I don't have much of a choice, do I? Think about it."

He was, but not about her and her dilemmas. He had lost a day somewhere, that was what was important, twenty-four hours of his life passed away in some drugged limbo. Things done, things said (he was sweating again) and they could never, ever be recaptured with any certainty.

At that moment, a dusty bulb on the wall – something he hadn't noticed – commenced flashing, red – off, red – off, red . . . They both saw it at the same time.

Nan said, "Ach, let him wait," but there was no way of ignoring that summons, for Billy Bonner himself had materialised in the room, his impatience beating regularly like a pulse. She encircled his calves with a moist grip. "Let me give you *something*," she pleaded with him. "Five minutes more . . ."

Everything about this outside world was cock-eyed, he told himself, including the roles of the men and women in it. He was looking about for the towel while prising this woman's flesh from his own, conscious of its potency to ensnare, with its warm, smooth difference. She began to weep, an inevitability after all that gin.

He said, "Thanks all the same, but it wouldn't be any good." He then followed it with something equally limp – like his equipment. "I'm not myself," he excused, pulling away.

He had wandered somehow on to a set where farce was in progress – everything pointed to it – and now he must struggle back into the costume they had provided for him, those same jokers who had stage-managed everything else for him this far. If he was to be their clown, he decided, then he would fulfil his function. Forgetting his nakedness, he proceeded to pull on the new pair of jazzy underpants (another of their little touches) then hopping as his trousers went on top of them.

Nan sobbed on the couch. They now ignored one another. The bulb, too, on the wall had its own concern. It chivvied them, a bit of coloured glass and filament, blinking.

When he had dressed himself and he was panting – nothing reminds a man more than that, how ill he's been – he felt sorry for the woman and her wretchedness. It was good to feel something

61

for someone other than himself again. "Thanks all the same," he said. One of his shoes was too tight, something he hadn't noticed before. "Maybe some other time ..."

She looked at him, her face a mess, then, as if reading what went through his mind, put a hand up to her cheek in a pathetic, tidying gesture. "I must look terrible."

On cue, he quickly said, "Not at all. I should be so lucky." It seemed an odd thing for him to say, foreign, yet never when it came from an actor's mouth.

"Here," she said, dipping into her handbag. "Take one."

He put the pink card carefully into his breast pocket. He didn't know what to say, so looked up at the winking bulb. "Somebody's finger must be getting tired."

Nan laughed, a bitter laugh. "Don't you believe it. He just loves it." Then, "See you around, big boy. I hope." She didn't mean it like that, but, none the less, he felt the old chill steal back again.

Inside his clown's suit, his bones felt fragile. The room and the woman in it seemed suddenly comfortable and comforting to him. He remembered how he had ached for a bed to lie on. The one in the middle of the room had been there all along for the taking, the woman too, sitting on it, now turned away from him.

He said, "Cheerio, Nan," closing the door slowly on the memory of her bare, unblemished back, then went down the stairs with equal reluctance to face Billy Bonner's grinning mug.

8

THE WIND ON THE BROW of the hill blew out Galloway's last match, and with it, his chance of a quiet smoke by himself. His oath startled a bird from almost under his feet. It went straight up as though on strings, for larks infested this place. He swore again, less loudly this time, although there was nothing and no one around to take a blind bit of notice. Bogs and bareness surrounded him, and back at the house in the hollow were those two saps who giggled at everything he said, and the ghost of a man in the corner who made him even more uneasy with his silences. Escape from the trio was the reason he had climbed up here in the first place, for by no stretch of the imagination could he ever be considered a lover of Nature. All of that out there disgusted him. He didn't know the reason, but it did. The space and the emptiness made him feel like an ant, so perhaps that was it. He ground savagely downwards with the heel of his boot, as though expecting to see a rush of the species come out of the earth. Instead, a thick brown liquid welled up and quickly filled the hollow he had formed.

He sat down on an old oil drum – that, at least, was from a world he knew – and stared seawards, facing into the breeze. It was evening, the land was cooling, air was drawn in, or so he had read somewhere, or remembered from something some boring teacher had once said. He could see Scotland, the Mull – his namesake – a low navy stripe along the top of the paler sea. It should have been a foreign country across there, different habits, language, people of another colour even, but it wasn't, it was the same – faces, voices and this identical waste of rock, whins and wet muck wherever you set your foot down. Galloway smiled bitterly. He could hardly be said to have travelled very far.

The first time he had made the crossing had been by ferry, breakfasting with the other lorry drivers, while, down in the hold, his own rig had enough wrapped sticks stowed away in secret to send up an entire fleet. Not that that ever bothered him, even being stopped. A charmed life was what he had led then. And still do, he told himself fiercely. But, then again, if you have to keep on telling yourself . . .

Hunched on his rusty throne, Ned Galloway surveyed the bleak prospect. He felt lost without the comforting embrace of bricks and mortar, his bolt-holes and short cuts, all that lore of the city he had acquired in his still brief life. He was thinking too much again. All this emptiness encouraged it. It took the action out of a man, the quickness. As a child he had never any desire to visit the country, fish streams or moon around camp-fires like the others. Holiday excursions were a torment, until he was old enough to avoid them. He gloried in the musty dark of flea-pits, breathed deeply the sooty reek of the close and the tip, his lungs, like his fingernails, a rich satisfying black.

From his battered Old Holborn tin, he took out a pinch of grass and put it into his mouth. He chewed it to a moist cud. Some could get a quicker buzz this way, but it never worked out like that for him. Still, it was something to do, even though it did make him look like a bloody cow. He replenished the quid. Wasteful. And not all that easy to come by either, for Bonner and his crowd were very hard-line about smoking. They seemed to think it was more Protestant to spend their time trying to get inside a bottle.

Like all smokers, Galloway held the other habit in contempt. He had started off that way himself, until he tried his first joint in Cyprus. After that it was smokes or nothing. Nothing since had measured up to that tawny, beautiful weed the fishermen brought back from Africa. One night, in a taverna in his civvies, he got as high as a kite. Smoke followed smoke. He began to hear tom-toms; they played recognisable rhythms. Convinced he really had negro blood, he began to strip, searching for tell-tale pigmentation. When most of his duds were on the floor, the owner of the dive, and his two sons, laid their oily hands on him. After that everything seemed to go into slow-motion. Papa landed up on his kebab burner, number one wog son went through a plate-glass window, and wog son two got a skewer through his cummerbund. The odd thing was that he felt no animosity towards any of them. His mates told him, afterwards, he had a broad smile on his face from start to finish, the reason why they hesitated to interfere – *they* said. If he'd been pissed, he reflected, instead of stoned, he might still be in khaki, but, as it was, the old man had a down on drugs, and so it was a dishonourable discharge or nothing. They even gave him a piece of paper, in case he might ever want to frame it.

After that he drifted about the streets back home until someone in a pub one night casually asked if he'd like to make some bread helping the cause. It was as sloppy as that. Some stranger in a greasy anorak, and an accent you could slice with a knife, offered him a wad to run some gelly across the water. At the time the miners were bringing up a stick apiece in their lunch tins every shift. That was how he had fallen in with Bonner and his mob in the first place. Then, of course, the heat came on and he found himself stranded on the wrong side of the Burn. Story so far. New readers start here . . .

He dug his clenched hands deeper into the pockets of his old leather jacket, for the wind had an edge to it by now. But it was better shivering up here than having to put up with the tiresome threesome below. Not only did he resent the company, he burned still at the thought of being given charge of this stupid operation. It just wasn't his line, he had once more reminded Bonner. *Get yourself another nanny.* Bonner smiled at the word, then put on his serious face, coming the old soldier yet again about there being nobody else he could trust, nobody with sufficient savvy etcetera etcetera. Why don't you just knock him off, then, suggested Galloway, and be done with it? Bonner's face changed colour. "There's no question of that. Don't even *think* about it. There are implications here you wouldn't even begin to under-stand. I mean" – quickly, putting a hand on his arm – "*strategies.*" Billy Bonner and Henry Kissinger; who'd have thought they would have so bloody much in common?

At that moment, borne on the wind, came a sound like that of a lawn-mower, only such things don't fly. Helicopters – army ones – do, however, and there was nothing but to sit and wait for it to come peering down at him. They might take him for a rustic. He chewed steadily. The khaki dragonfly clattered closer. There were two men in it, in their jungle-jims. Galloway thought of waving, then decided against the idea. It was out of character for someone dressed as he was, bomber-jacket, jeans, boots. He kept his gaze fixed instead on the darkening ribbon on the horizon – land of his fathers. The two squaddies in the chopper overhead wanted him to look up, but he wouldn't please them. He hated them all the more vehemently because once he had been one himself. He could smell them, their stale sweat, the oil that never came off your hands or your uniform. When you stink like a pig, you become one. He spat and the hovering machine shied as though at his action. Then it slid away at a shallow angle across the terrain. *Home to base, home to base. Nothing to report, except one local yokel communing with his Maker. Over and out . . .*

He remembered his Troodos days. If it was in the open, it was either a wog or his donkey. Strange how he had now changed sides. One of life's little ironies, or some such crap.

Galloway watched the ungainly machine until it shrank to the size of just one more homing bird. He waited until it disappeared, however, for he knew how rapidly those flying oil-cans could come wheeling back. Anything that moved always attracted their attention, and he felt he had made a bad enough move, as it was, by being spotted in the first place. It wasn't like him, he told himself, taking risks. He was angry now. His face felt inflamed, despite the breeze from all that expanse of sea.

When at last he stood up, his backside was numb as well, from sitting so long on rusty metal. He rubbed his seat vigorously, then dealt the offending drum a kick as an afterthought. It didn't seem to help; his mood had now become one only to be eased by retaliation of some sort. Inside his waistband was the instrument, but it might as well have been a toy for all the use he was to make of it. They gave him a weapon, but no target.

He began walking back to where they were holding the prisoner. A crazy scheme grew in Galloway's head. Why not knock off all three, whispered an inner voice, blame it on the big fellow making a break for it, then confusion within four walls?

66

There would be plenty of time to make it look plausible. On second thoughts, why bother? A phone call would ensure that the law got there first. He could then get back in time to watch the whole thing on television with Bonner; listen to the usual spiel from the usual youth with the microphone. "Another spate of seemingly motiveless killings in this tragic countryside, where death can strike at any time." Yawn, yawn . . .

He went down the hill towards the tin-roofed shack in the hollow, his feet sliding on grass. Old car bodies glinted in the dying sun. The scene looked lifeless, as it was meant to be. He halted for a moment, surveying the disorder, half hoping for a sign that those inside had gone against his wishes – an opening in the curtains, rising smoke – but there was nothing. Blood-letting had now gone from his mind. Like sex, the idea of it could be just as good sometimes. All it left behind was a slight after-taste, like something on the tongue.

He reached the house and when he opened the door, using his boot to give those inside a start – he had the only weapon after all – Duff and Blackie were still playing pontoon. They didn't even look up. Galloway stared at the empty chair where the prisoner should have been, his mouth going dry. Radio One droned softly from the portable on the table.

He shouted at them, "*Where is he? Where is he?*" and, if it hadn't been for the repetition, he could have sworn neither would have stirred.

Duff pointed at the door. The albino, on his feet, stuttered, "He's only having a sh– sh–," but Galloway was running out once more into the late afternoon air, unzipping his jacket to get at the heavy police special wedged in his belt.

He moved in among wrecks of cars, treading on countless grains of glass from their windscreens. It reminded him suddenly of a film he'd once seen and, remembering how the unarmed actor had waylaid the villain, he crept forward cautiously. He had been careless, perhaps all along, in not realising how desperate his adversary must be. For the first time he saw someone fighting for his life, because, despite Bonner's denials, there had to be only one outcome for the man he was now hunting; a bullet with his name on it. He felt eager at the thought of the clincher being so near, began to sweat a little as he always did. It was all so close in there among the rusting carcases. No wind moved. He felt the heat all that metal, rubber and splintered glass had absorbed so patiently over the preceding hours. The sun was weaker, certainly, but now it seemed to beat off every available surface and into his eyes. He crouched lower, moving his head from side to side like an animal. He glanced upwards too, because ambush, if it came, might well drop from above. Once or twice he was able to look through the empty windows of several cars at once, or gain a vista along corridors of trampled grass. He had hopes of a glimpse of feet and lower leg.

But the confrontation, when it came, was not as he had expected. In a small clearing, chosen carefully, even fastidiously, Galloway was to recognise, there squatted the man he had invested with such ferocity. Around his ankles were his pants; beside him, on the grass, a square of newspaper. That detail, like the privacy of the setting, disconcerted Galloway most, for some strange reason. He stared at the man, and the man stared back. They were like two survivors of a wreck, meeting on this island of turf.

Finally, Galloway coughed, and took the excuse it offered to look away. It was weakness, and he knew it. He felt angry with himself. He wanted to do something crude, humiliating. Instead, he found himself pretending interest in the closest object at hand, a furry steering-wheel in one of the cars. When he could bear the fraud of that no longer, he went and waited on the far side of the upturned vehicle. Now he felt confused. It wasn't the first time. This man, a little way off, unhurriedly crapping, seemed to have it in his power to make him respond in such a fashion. Why was that? Galloway sought some answer, leaning up against the now cooling bodywork. In the past there had been others who had spread a similar nervousness in him, teachers, ministers, men in the services, with moustaches and the voices to match. They looked at him in a certain way, and nearly always were half-smiling. Now, if someone were to call him Jock – the name and the smile going together – he knew what his reaction would be. He fingered the butt of the .38, then drew it from his trousers. Cradling the weapon in both hands, he allowed the pleasure its weight and touch always afforded to take hold. He laid the barrel to his cheek, sniffing. He felt better already.

"Do you need a hand back there?" he called out.

That was more like it, he told himself, more like the old Ned. He began to think of further witticisms for the moment when the other would emerge, buttoning his breeks in that slow way he had of doing everything. How could he ever have allowed such a clapped-out relic to get under his skin? Crapped out. He laughed, hoping the sound would carry. Well-being swam in his veins now. Perhaps it was the grass he had been chewing, perhaps not, but whatever it was he now held the nub of things. The word "slow" was what counted, the telling one. He chuckled at his own cleverness. That lack of urgency in everything the big fellow did, his *slowness*, yes, that was it. He had allowed himself to be fooled – he didn't care about that now – seeing it as a sign of some strength, when all along it had nothing to do with character at all. Instead – and here he rummaged for something in his other pocket – it came out of a bottle. He held the eye-dropper up, so that the sun caught its content. The liquid was clear, like water, odourless too, as he had noted each time a gentle pressure had released its single tear into the big man's drink. Three times a day he had dutifully squeezed that rubber bulb. An analgesic, Billy Bonner had said, highly concentrated, and don't let him see you putting it in his tea. He doesn't realise how sick he really is, and none of us is exactly like Doctor Kildare, are we, eh? Always the grin on the face, and the pat on the arm.

Galloway gently shook the little phial, then unscrewed the cap and touched his own tongue with the wet tip of its stem. Tasteless. As innocent as tap-water. Some time he would like to find out for himself the nature of this potion that could make a man run down like an old clock. Tick-tock. He swung the glass dropper to and fro, delighted at the darting of his mind. He could throw this tiny toy away, now hot in his hand, or he could empty it out on the grass at his feet; the choice was his. One thing was certain, however, he was not going to dose the big man further. Bonner's "strategies" were his own affair. He had to admit he also liked the idea of being a saboteur, almost as much as he liked the word, which had surfaced suddenly like a bauble from the depths.

There was something else too, of course, harder to put into words, even though it had nagged at him for some considerable time. From the outset, this man, a few paces off, busy about his call of nature, had been something of an obsession to him. Like it or not, it was true; he was in the mood for honesty. Everything he had been told had prepared him for something, someone, larger than life. He should have known better, of course. It had happened before, his own imagination adding a dimension here, extra colouring there. They stretched in a long line behind him, he reflected, almost sadly, all those demolition jobs. Yet to be fair (strange word for him) this one, beyond, hadn't had a real chance, the contest all too one-sided, thanks to what he held in his hand. Three times a day, before meals, but usually with, all those droplets secretly milked into his tea. They each had their own mug just as if they were work-mates. Funny that. Galloway thought it would be interesting to give the big man an opportunity to show his mettle, that's if he had any, and strangely, half-hoping himself now that he had.

As for these precious knockout drops, he had a better use for them than watering the grass. He thought of Duff and the albino cast in the role of two sleeping beauties, fitting punishment for their carelessness, and laughed long and heartily.

Silver emerged buttoning up, as the other imagined he might, while blinking into the setting sun.

"Welcome back to the land of the living, dad!" shouted Galloway, at the sight of him, and he kept laughing all the way back to the shack in the hollow.

9

"ANOTHER FAN OF YOURS! Aren't we the popular boy, then?" Bonner shouting above the din and pushing the one they all called Tiffany into the chair directly opposite.

The nightmare had taken a further turn, for facing him was a slim man, heavily rouged and powdered, and wearing a low-cut evening frock. He was smiling at him with parted lips. They glistened with some wet and shiny stuff – a kiss to be avoided at all costs. The thought didn't strike him as bizarre, for his only salvation lay now, he had decided, in appearing to accept each new abnormality as and when it presented itself.

"What an honour. What a privilege," the stranger kept repeating in a voice which had no trace of effeminacy; his jowls, beneath the Panstick, were dark, hair curled strongly from beneath the padded bust, and there was a tattoo on his right forearm. The prisoner recognised the faded blue swift so popular at one time.

His own head was beginning to reel with the noise. At the far end of the room a three-piece group throbbed manfully, yet could barely be heard above the hectic conviviality of those yelling and drinking at the scattered tables. As far as he could gather, they were in a night-haunt called The Loft. The name, he had been given to understand, had its origin back in the days when the place had been a working-men's pigeon club. But, as Bonner had put it, with his customary grin, "The only birds you'll see around here, Silver, old son, are the ones drinking Snowballs," and, of course, there they were, the wives, the girl-friends and daughters, dressed to kill, while their menfolk swam in a sea of strong drink. All faces in the room were flushed and moist, laughing mouths opened with a terrifying mobility; he felt unease at the sights and sounds pressing upon him.

The painted person in the sheath dress opposite was leaning forward too, scent flowing from him in waves. "The next number is dedicated to you, Silver," reaching below the table and coming up with a woman's blonde wig. It sat on the table between them for a moment, a massive lacquered nest, a parody of every other coiffure in the room. Then Tiffany placed it on his own cropped head.

"See!" he said, with justifiable pride, for, indeed, there was some sort of transformation. The prisoner instantly recognised any one of a handful of heavy country-music queens, for all had that unmistakable and identical look.

It seemed that his speciality was Dolly Parton, the hair-piece stuck with cheap stones made that clear enough, but, for Silver, he would sing a Tammy Wynette hit. He stood up and kissed the fingertips of both hands towards Silver. The action, like his appearance, was yet one more parody, this time of the film routine where the torch singer embarrasses the baldest man in the night-club. It caused the people around – as in the movie – to catcall and stamp their feet. Faces beamed their goodwill, further drinks were ordered to swell the ranks of those already on the table. The man in the unfashionably loose suit felt himself shrinking even deeper into its itchy folds. Once he had been as snappy a dresser as the best of these in their chalkstripes and polyesters. Maroon, as a colour, seemed to be favoured, he noted out of tired eyes. It did nothing for the complexion. He remembered the only beautiful thing he had seen since he had first been bundled back into this savage, unreal world; the sight of a woman's naked and quite flawless back.

72

And now all the heads had swung to the small stage, the trio silenced, and a solitary pink spotlight trained on the glittering figure standing there. Applause broke out. It seemed spontaneous, genuinely admiring, especially from the women. Even the hardest-faced among them looked sentimental for a moment. The prisoner saw several dabbing at their eyes.

Tiffany spoke; a microphone had appeared in her jewelled fist. "This song is dedicated to all our loved ones Behind the Wire" – a roaring approbation burst forth – "but especially tonight, to one of them . . . who is no longer there."

All faces turned towards the man in the baggy suit. They bayed their love for him and, at the sound, he felt he had become their property. At his side Bonner was also applauding. A thin cigar he bit between his teeth helped conceal his cynical smile. He clapped him viciously on the shoulders, and the prisoner felt manhandled in more ways than one. And now all were calling on him to speak (*"Silver! Silver!"*) Tiffany graciously extending her very own silvery wand, out over the heads to where he sat hunched. He was theirs, now they desired something from his repertoire of tricks. Heat and noise and the cigarette haze making an almost solid cone of the spotlight's beam, and such fleshy faces. Above everything else, they made him feel like the refugee he truly was.

Yet at the same time his paralysis, he was telling himself, was crazy. He could surely muster something, anything to satisfy this mob. A string of grunts would suffice. He recalled briefings and rallying speeches in that ordered world he had come from, his own voice confidently ringing out not so long ago. But now he was trembling, and had been taken hard with yet another sweating fit. All his suspicions as to his state pointed to what he had been pressed to drink, for Bonner had been insistent with his hospitality ever since they had arrived. The rounds came remorselessly, enormous measures of almost neat spirits in wet tumblers. The table was already awash, the knees of his cheap trousers soaked with the overflow. He wondered how Bonner managed to keep his own suiting intact. No mean feat to remain as spruce as he did in a shebeen such as this one.

"*Speech! Speech!*" They were calling on him still. "*Speech! Speech!*" The single, repeated word, coming from all those roaring throats, seemed absurdly formal. More and more he was finding derangement in almost everything. Or was the seed in himself? He looked over the array of alcohol at the joker opposite. Planted by this agent in the natty two-piece and matching shirt-and-tie set? The prisoner made a resolve that if he must drink for the sake of appearances, then it must only be from the glass of a stranger.

Bonner raised his own and winked at him, just as the chorus of voices all around him had begun to falter. The juncture was delicate. In another moment a sullen mood might easily take over, then that well-known decline set in. Already the prisoner could hear the sound of breaking glass as a finale to the evening. He hadn't been so long out of circulation not to remember what Saturday nights meant to his people. But Billy Bonner was on his feet to save the day. Hands upraised, he appealed to the crowd, "Brothers and sisters. I'm sure you'll forgive our guest of honour if he declines saying a few words. He's had a trying time, as you can see –" The prisoner felt a multitude of bleary eyes trying to focus on his condition. A maudlin sigh of sympathy went up. Several women, and not a few of the men, tried to get close enough to embrace him, but were prevented by the creaking leather armour of Bonner's bodyguards, who had risen suddenly from adjacent tables.

Bonner now dropped his hand on to the prisoner's shoulder. "Comrades, Silver is only here tonight to demonstrate his solidarity, for he's still – under doctor's orders." It was that phrase which seemed most sinister. "A big hand, folks, for a very brave man who's come through a lot!"

The cheers were all for him; he was their hero. All those faces turned in his direction assured the man in the ill-fitting suit that he had only to ask and his slightest wish would be granted.

When Bonner dropped back down into his seat, he said to him, "I need to go to the toilet." For a second the self-congratulation in those pale eyes died, then came flooding back again. "Sure. The little boys' room is back there." He waved a hand towards the rear. "Young Terry will show you. And Terry – make sure Silver has privacy. Okay?" The young heavyweight nodded grimly, and they set off through the tables.

Their passage was slow. Many hands reached out to grasp and detain affectionately; one woman managed to wet his cheek with a kiss, despite Terry's roughness. No one seemed to take offence, however; most were already drunk in a brutally anaesthetised fashion. At last the bruising passage was completed, and while the prisoner closed himself into one of the lavatory stalls his guardian simply leaned his broad back against the outer door. As he squatted there where the lighting was not quite so glaring the prisoner could hear the steady munching of those strong young jaws. Young Terry, as everybody seemed to call him, dipped into a bag of crisps with the greedy relish of a schoolboy. The prisoner had noticed the oily state of his fingers as he manipulated their progress to this toilet. He seemed to delight in leaving their greasy imprint on everyone and everything that barred their way, the sort of humour to go hand-in-hand with a juvenile enjoyment of jokes about bodily functions. Certainly he would find it hard to resist adding his own contribution to the back of this door, decided the man contemplating the scrawls facing him. He let his eyes travel idly over them, deciding that the wit on display was greatly inferior to that which he was used to. Where he came from, men had, it seemed, almost infinite time on their hands. The best they could run to here was the old, "A Merry Xmas to all our Readers," the rest the usual boasts about weaponry and stamina. Someone called Big Denise seemed to be the resident bicycle. For some reason all those pencilled testimonials made him think of the girl in the massage parlour. It was the second time that perfect pelt and the memory of its touch had stirred him strangely. He stood up to wipe himself, surprised and greatly shocked at his own arousal.

Then, close to the top of the door, he saw his own name. *Silver Rules O.K.*, he read. And there it was again, in another place. In a moment, he was discovering it all over the painted surface, hidden away among the graffiti like some shy but persistent plant. It made him sit down again on the covered seat. Even Bonner couldn't have stage-managed this, he told himself.

All those years locked away, he had of course realised that his reputation and exploits had become popular property. Any man would have found some of that to his taste. Propaganda value was an important aspect too, of course. Early on, he had recognised just how desperate the craving for symbols and symbolism could be. In his own way he himself had become one of those, without being consulted. It had been the least one could do for patriotism. Then. But gradually, as time passed in that other enclosed existence, he had changed, he knew he had, the outside world seeming further and further away, alien in its irregular daily pulse, its lack of inevitability. It began to seem like a crazy planet out there, beyond the chicken wire, with politicians roaring on, off, hot and cold, ordinary people in the grip of violent and unreasonable action for its own sake. He didn't of course announce his disenchantment, or let slip any signals, if he could help it; there were still far too many around him who he knew could, or would, never alter. They continued to live vicariously on reported exploits from the other side, drilling and training for a day when they too would be at large. He himself, as their superior, encouraged the illusion; more, he drove them without mercy in all weathers on the tiny recreation ground. The guards always watched with a mixture of emotions – half mocking, half uneasy, at all the seriousness unleashed by those wooden weapons and makeshift uniforms. No, he, Silver, certainly couldn't *fully* believe in all that toy soldiery, nor in a day of reckoning either, when the perimeter fencing would fall flat like Jericho before the marching feet of Compounds Seventeen and Eighteen, intent on inheriting the earth.

His motives were simple, if the truth were to be known. Let them have their dreams, he had decided, if it kept them not so much happy as disciplined, for that word had come to stand for sanity with him. There was still enough of the madhouse inside the wire even when it seemed that all the lunatics might well be out and about on the other side. Sanity, survival – his own – depended on his fellow inmates. He had begun to feel like an old man of late, set down among a batch of dangerous and unruly boys, so he harangued them and he chivvied them, inventing more and more elaborate schemes of exhaustion. The pretence of it all sapped him as well. They were united in that respect, at least, every man jack in his bunk after lights out, sleeping like a dead thing. He thought of those rows of stretched men, their mingled breath filling the long, low huts. His own bed, apart a little, naturally, in its curtained alcove, would be empty now at this time. The prisoner looked around the confines of this other cubicle he now crouched in, with its muted sounds of plumbing. He felt more confined here and now than he had ever been. The bolt was across, certainly, which should have tendered him some little comfort, but didn't, of course. He fixed his gaze on it and, sure enough, saw it start to vibrate.

Then Young Terry's voice reached him, surprisingly restrained, through the door. "Have you finished?" The prisoner stirred noisily and flushed the cistern.

At the wash-basin he immersed his hands, after soaping them

76

from the glass dispenser. It was a simple luxury to have clean hands for the first time, he calculated, since he had been taken from hospital. Terry watched without expression and, if he was impatient, it didn't show. He proferred his open bag of crisps. "They're smoky bacon." The prisoner shook his head, thinking of his hands.

Then Terry said, eyeing him as he buried them deeply in the loop of the roller towel, "*We* don't think you're all that fucking marvellous."

"Too bad," the prisoner heard himself say. His voice was quietly offhand. Just right, he thought to himself, as he spun out his toilet. A small victory surely, of some kind. Two tiny words, but it was their tone that was so important. Had the other noticed? Brother-in-law most certainly would have. And now he wanted Terry to continue, not just out of curiosity, but from a desire to test his own mettle. He hoped his idling before the mirror would lead to further disclosures, and he was right.

"Billy says you're a back number. Billy says," – and here he paused, as if trying to recall word-for-word something he had once overheard – "Billy says you've outlived your usefulness."

The face in the mirror showed no change; the eyes, the mouth, those features, which should have reacted to that last chilling phrase, betrayed nothing. It was as though he were watching someone else's reflection in the slightly tinted glass.

"Did Billy tell you to tell me that?"

The other fell silent, but there was a frantic outburst of rustling followed by much chewing. The prisoner knew that the young thug was now afraid he had spoken out of turn.

"Never mind, Terry, I'll just have to live with it," he told him.

He was almost nonchalant now in front of the glass, putting those finishing touches to his appearance which would not have been considered out of place in someone half his age. He remembered peacock nights-out from the past, and all the activity before a foot was ever placed on a dance floor. It was like waltzing in the biggest perfume department in the world.

Then they went out through the door back into that other dim, smoke-filled hell-hole. The noise seemed to have a clout of its own, and, in a moment, all his new-found courage had ebbed away. Young Terry began cutting a swathe through the dense jam, his course set undeviatingly for their table. He followed close enough to that shiny black bulk to have the smell of new leather in his nostrils, until Bonner and his party loomed up. His seat was waiting for him, and he dropped into it with relief.

Bonner said, "It hasn't been the same without you. No fun without Punch, you know." He slapped him on the knee, and the action, as well as his tone, was oddly affectionate. The others around the table seemed to share the feeling, for even Young Terry was grinning back at him in that moment. It could have been a fresh ploy, concocted in his absence, but then, again, the prisoner thought not. He pretended to drink when a full glass was pressed on him, he even managed to summon up an answering smile across its rim, and Bonner was moved to exclaim, "Solidarity. We must all stick together. Solidarity. Didn't I say it? Didn't I?"

The others nodded. Their solemnity was out of place in this frantic happidrome. People at other tables seemed oblivious to the broken glass underfoot and the damage to their clothes from spilled beer and spirits. A woman, not too far distant, was about to be sick, but couldn't get up from her chair. No one else seemed to notice except himself. With an effort he pulled his gaze away from that face filling with dulled panic.

"After all, we have more in common than we have in –" The word Bonner was searching for didn't exist, or, if it did, it hovered beyond the reaches of his vocabulary. He finished the sentence instead with a flourish of his cheroot. Its dead tip caught the sleeve of one of his companions who pretended not to notice.

"It won't come to drastic measures. It doesn't have to."

The prisoner realised he was talking, or rather, thinking aloud, about him, his situation. There were just the two of them now; the others, as though divining the true state of affairs, for Bonner's eyes had lost their focus, withdrew tactfully to their own serious drinking.

Again came that grip on his knee and a chair being moved closer. "The differences aren't irreconcilable. Old comrades. That must stand for something. Eh?" He felt himself nodding. "Things could – *can* be worked out. To suit everybody." Bonner smiled then. He continued to smile into space, and, for the next minute or so, the prisoner bore a shifting pressure on his thigh in lieu of words. Sentiment was rising in this man like a warm and spreading flood, and tears could not be ruled out. He recognised the treacherous condition, for he had wallowed there himself, and so had learnt to distrust it in others, particularly in someone like Bonner. In the morning, memory would bring him a swift remorse, then the determination to be even more ruthless in the future. In any pogrom that might follow he saw himself already as first victim.

No wonder they despised him. He despised himself – for his inertia. Every so often, a creeping blight, not dissimilar, would overtake certain men in the Compounds, a paralysis of the will that left them curled up under their blankets, knees to chin, for as long as they might be allowed to remain like that. The condition was common enough to make the rest fear it as something infectious. For days on end they might well cover up for such a man, by calling his name at roll-call, but, just as easily, they might also kick him from his bed, driving him before them to the sick bay for more Valium. That particular *cafard* of the spirit, thank God, had been spared him. In others, it was something he knew about, but chose to ignore, just as the guards turned their eyes, in much the same way, from the wooden weapons. The irony was, of course, that had been finally brought down with something very like it, at this point, here and now, on the *outside*, among all these armour-plated idiots.

He looked about him. The middle-aged woman, someone's mother, had now fallen face downwards on to the table. Perhaps she hadn't been sick after all; perhaps, mercifully, she had only passed out. As before, he seemed to be the only one to notice her state. Her husband stared glassily before him. What were they doing in this place anyway, Darby and Joan, mutton dressed as lamb?

At that moment a muffled reverberation burst out (it made him start) followed by a cruel, electronic whine. Bonner's friends laughed at his panic. He grinned weakly back.

Bonner, out of his reverie by now, said, "Your nerves are bad, Silver. You should take something for them." As though sharing some private joke, the others laughed even more uproariously than before and the prisoner had to curb himself from joining in. He had fallen about as low as he could go, that was clear. Their faces seemed to be bobbing before him. He thought of Hallowe'en masks. He wanted suddenly to crush those hollow turnip-heads. It was a feeling that surprised and, in a way, pleased him, something secret of his own, a brief flare of spirit.

The sounds, of course, came from the stage and the microphone returned now to Tiffany's hand. It was back on its stand, but the drag-queen held and caressed it in such a way that the crowd opened its throat with delight. The great eyelashes fluttered and the painted mouth puckered in mock distress at such crudity. Then, tiring of the pantomime with the silver stem, she launched into "Stand By Your Man." By the time the chorus had arrived, it was obvious to everyone in the place who the sentiments were intended for. Bonner was nudging him, there were broad winks from the turnip-tops, a multitude of other heads turned unsteadily in his direction.

"Stand by your man,
Give him two arms to cling to,
And something warm to come to, when nights are cold and lonely,
Stand by your man,
And show the world you love him,
Keep giving all the love you can,
Stand by your man –"

Tiffany faltered suddenly and broke off. She was looking out over all their heads at something or someone no one else could see in the dark recesses near the door. Then, in a harsh, masculine voice, she bellowed into the mike, "It's a raid! The army's here!"

Hiking up her expensive gown, she jumped from the stage, and started pushing for the single door marked Exit. The crowd gasped. No one moved. Then one woman screamed, and the high sound released a bass thunder of panic. Glasses smashed, tables overturned. The band were hurriedly ripping out the wires from their equipment. Then some uninspired and nameless idiot pulled a master-switch somewhere, and they were plunged into almost total darkness. Silver heard voices around him calling helplessly, "Billy! Billy!" but only the glowing end of cigar told him that Bonner still hadn't moved.

He thought quickly, this may be the only opportunity you'll ever be offered, so run now, for god's sake. But then he considered – in which direction? Towards the men in khaki?

Points of light were beginning to spring up as people struck matches. In Montreal, the papers said, a dance-hall fire had started from just such a source. Was it forty or fifty who had been incinerated then? He felt someone grip his arm, as though reading his thoughts. "I should have known about this. I should have been *told*." He knew the voice was Bonner's, but it was hard to recognise, so husky with emotion had it become.

Then another voice came from the dark, unmistakably Terry's. "Billy, what about the takings?"

"Never mind what's in the till, stupid. Get this christian out of here."

"But what about you?"

They both heard Bonner sigh heavily. "Get him out of here before he's spotted. And don't worry, the lights won't come on again till I'm ready."

The prisoner felt the restraining hand on his sleeve give a final squeeze. "You're becoming a liability, you know that, old sport?" quietly confidential for his ears alone, then, "Au revoir – for the time being."

The sweating bulk of Young Terry came close. For a second time that night he was to be placed in his charge. This time, however, as they laboured through the unseen drifts of cursing, sprawling men and hysterical women, Terry kicking out before him with great good humour, he was gripped as close as any dancing-partner. The smell of fried potatoes clung now to both of them.

At the toilet door they heard the unmistakable tones of Aldershot rising above the clamour, and coming from a loud-hailer. "There's no need to panic! Stay where you are! This is merely a routine search-and-find operation. Please don't panic, I say!"

Beams of light were already beginning to stitch the darkness, as army torches sought their target. It was strange to realise that he himself was the reason for their being here. His spirits sank. His world, for what it was worth, was contracting steadily with each new turn of events. It seemed barely possible, but there it was.

Still in Young Terry's embrace, he allowed himself to be bundled into the echoing darkness of the toilets, then guided past the basins towards a hitherto concealed door in the far wall. Beyond was open air and, above, the night sky. There were stars. The prisoner breathed in deeply and Young Terry said, "I hope you're fit. We have a few back walls to climb. Let's travel."

10

THE REST OF THAT NIGHT, or what little was left of it, he spent in yet another strange bed, yet this time the sheets were clean, strikingly so. He only wished he had been able to have a bath to do justice to their laundered purity. The old-fashioned mattress cupped him. It was like another era; the bed, the patchwork quilt, the chink of china when his foot strayed underneath. There were framed Bible texts on the walls and feminine toilet articles on a veneered dressing-table. Its mirror registered his surprise when he awoke, for he had gone to sleep in almost total dark. The blind was still pulled, but enough light poured in through its pale fabric for him to take in his surroundings. A smell of frying bacon rose from below. Last night he had mounted stairs. The woman of the house had led him by the hand, calling him "Son". He felt certain this must be her room. For a moment, lying in that woman's bed, it was as though the past days and nights, all his years in custody, for that matter, had been imagined, and now he had awoken at last. From some distant time he remembered such things, clean linen, the smell of lavender polish, someone cooking his breakfast. He heard church bells: those were real enough. If this dream were true, he told himself, there would be an ironed shirt hanging over the back of a chair.

He opened his eyes. In a heap on the floor lay his crumpled clown's outfit, the garish underpants they had supplied him, for amusement, draped like an obscenity on top.

Sunday, he thought. A week and almost a day at large. But how much longer could they hope to keep on shuttling him from place to place like this, from one safe house to the next? It came to him just how stretched Bonner's inventiveness must be by now. Last night's events must certainly have left him longing for a release from his burden. That whispered word "liability" returned. Naked under the bedclothes, the prisoner lay and pondered on these things. Yet his fate still seemed to him not his, but another's. How simple it would be to just lie here like this staring at the blind changing colour. Outside it must be a day of bright sun and fast-moving cloud. He thought of the churchgoers, girls in gloves holding on to their hats as the wind got up – from time to time the blind swayed. What if he rose, dressed himself and, moving carefully, reached the window? The drop to the ground shouldn't be too damaging. He knew these houses after all, their tiny yards. There might be a dustbin underneath, then again there might not. Why make obstacles? He saw himself running down that long back entry to freedom. Then the old despair returned, for where did freedom lie? It was a word fast becoming meaningless, a remnant of some buried language.

A banging came on the floorboards. It sounded as though someone below had taken up a broom handle. He lay sweating. The noise ceased and he swung bare legs out and on to the woman's rag rug. He imagined her appreciating its modest comfort on such mornings.

He had the hairless shanks of a pensioner. *Son*, she had called him. Self-pity moistened his eyes. Then, gripping the edges of the bed, he raised himself, waiting for the usual dizziness. It seemed less pronounced, a surprise; fewer too of those swirling motes in technicolour. He commenced a gentle kneading of his scalp, exploratory of that area the doctors had examined. Their touch had made him wince, so, remembering, he was careful. The pain seemed now to be localised, he noted. Whatever was the matter with him there, they had kept it from him – that is, if they had the chance to reach a diagnosis before he was bundled off. Ironic to let such a thing engage him at this time, he thought, studying his gaunt frame in the mirror. His loss of weight must surely constitute the best disguise of all, it came to him.

He began to dress. The reek of last night still clung to his heap of clothes on the linoleum. It was like pulling on someone else's dirty duds. Captivity had bred in him too much fastidiousness for his own good. At the same time he recognised how easily he might have swung to an opposite extreme. Nothing half-way about attitudes in that other existence. It was something he had noticed over the years.

There came a further muffled tattoo on the ceiling below and he began to hurry. All thought of escape via the window had departed now, but when he went to the door and found it unlocked, the absurdity of that earlier impulse struck home. They took it for granted, his keepers did, that he wouldn't make a run for it. Not now. Not at this stage of the game. For a moment he toyed with the idea of looking behind the blind just to see if the window had been barred, or even if he had been right about the entry below, then apathy took hold and directed him instead downstairs to face a further instalment of what fate held in store for him. In a way it wasn't completely unpleasant. It was like watching a dentist preparing his next relay of instruments. You knew they were scalpel-sharp and there might be blood, but the anaesthetic bathed you in its protective balm. He could almost hear Bonner's voice whisper, "You won't feel a thing, old hand, not a thing," as he closed the bedroom door.

In the kitchen below there was a blue haze of frying that stung the eyes. "Come and get it!" called out Young Terry. He was in the scullery waving a smoking pan over the gas. Then he carried in two plates heaped with the results of his cooking. The prisoner couldn't help noticing how disproportionate their contents happened to be. He felt glad in a way, for all appetite had flown at first sight of that fried mess, and the two thumbs gripping the edges of the china.

"Get stuck in. You're at your granny's."

Terry was wearing a soiled yellow T-shirt with *Southern Comfort* across its front. He hadn't shaved, and his mighty paps swung as he plunged his fork into his egg-yolks.

"Sauce?"

It seemed a grotesque gentility on his part, for the table at which they sat and ate had barely room enough for their two plates. A loaf, butter, marmalade and jam, pickles, ketchup, cake and biscuits, as well as the tea things, were dispersed across its surface, as though every cupboard in the place had been raided expressly for Terry's schoolboy greed. The prisoner thought of the woman. It was as well she wasn't here to see this. Blood-red gouts of sauce rained down on the plate opposite, Terry using the heel of his hand on the base of the bottle. Then he started wolfing in earnest. The prisoner watched. When the other had finished, he pushed his own untouched plate across, and Terry barely paused for breath before embarking on that as well. Not a word had been spoken throughout the entire meal, but eventually a satisfied belch broke the silence, and the young giant opposite commenced picking his teeth with a spent match.

After a time he spoke. "My cooking not up to your usual standard, is that it?"

"I don't feel hungry."

There was a pause.

"You're a right bloody puke, and no mistake, aren't you, Silver?"

The eyes opposite had retreated into their fleshy recesses. Fat young bastard, thought the prisoner, but he wasn't angry, just tired and cynical. It looked as though he was in for a continuation of last evening's needling. Well, perhaps he might just turn the blade himself, just once, or twice. Pigs did squeal, didn't they?

"What weight are you, Terry son?"

The bulk opposite shifted in the widow's best chair. "Why? Are you concerned?"

"Not me. But *you* should be. You won't make thirty."

"I'm fit, I tell you."

"But for what?" It was childish but cheering that he hadn't forgotten any of that old street-corner repartee.

"When did *you* last take a dekko in the mirror?"

"I've been thin for years," he heard himself lie. "You know, I could take three stones off you with no bother in a month, if I had you inside."

"*Inside?*" brayed the other. "*Inside?* Do you really believe you're going back? To your nice wee holiday-camp?"

The prisoner felt the thrust. It cut deep. "Who's talking of going back?" His voice held. "I'm on the *outside*, thanks to Billy. Free. Even you must understand what the word means."

Terry merely grinned at him. The prisoner thought, even this brainless young specimen knows the score. They all do, down to the last and the lowest. He got up from the table and went over to the room's only easy-chair which faced the television set. Under the cushioned seat he knew there would be reading matter, there always was, and his groping hand found a sheaf of periodicals. He stared unseeingly at the dull cover of *The Christian Herald*.

Terry laughed. "Miss the prayer meetings back in Butlin's? Eh, Silver?"

"Why don't you go and wash the woman's dishes."

That angered him, for some strange reason. "I never washed a plate in my life!"

"That's too bad, Terry, for I'll have you on your knees scrubbing out latrines on your first day inside." Again that word triggered off a guffaw but he couldn't be wounded like that a second time. "Correction. *I* personally won't have the pleasure of watching you sweat into a bucket, but others will. For there's no doubt about it, that's where you're bound, sooner or later. At a guess, Terry son, I'd say sooner, with your brainpower. Up to now you've led a very charmed life."

There was silence in the room. He turned the pages, pretending interest in the grey print and the greyer stories of readers who had seen the light. It all came back to him, the religion of his youth. He had even been "saved" himself at one stage, he recalled, doing the rounds of all the tin tabernacles, a smug exhibitionist lying about his misguided past in front of each new congregation. The mingled smell of mothballs and peppermints rising instead of incense. He thought of the woman who might well be sitting in such a place at this moment. Of course, she was, damn it, with her hat and hymnal and her coin for the collection tucked inside her glove. But how could she lend her house and herself to all of this? Turning a blind eye. Out of fear? There was a lot of it about. Such a woman – for he could really see her now – would never use the Confidential Telephone. Such a woman never used any phone, for that matter. One of the submerged seven-eighths. He had used the image on one of his tape recordings. "Our sole aim must be to overturn the social iceberg, stand it on its head, a place in the sun for all those who have been in the depths for too long."

His thoughts had led him away from reality for a short space and now it reasserted itself angrily in the person of his overweight companion, for he was in a rage, of that there was no doubt. From the kitchen came the sounds of bad temper as cupboards and drawers were slammed. Young Terry was searching for something. Surely it couldn't be for more food, was his thought. The table looked like a battlefield. Then there came a final crash, unmistakably that made by the door of the oven. In his easy-chair, the prisoner laid down his paper in readiness. The time had arrived for that next instalment.

Terry stood in the doorway, one hand held behind his back, and now he brought it around slowly into view, all the time watching intently to catch the full effect of what was in his grasp.

"Do you know what *this* is?"

"No. Tell me."

The prisoner was thinking, if he cocks one of those hammers – or both – for his thumb is certainly big enough, I must rush him, there is no choice any more. But also going through his head was the idea of Terry thinking how sharp he was in hitting upon such a clever cache for his surprise packet, then forgetting where he had put it.

"Aren't you a bit old to be playing with toys at your age?"

"This is no toy, and I'm not playing."

The dialogue was vintage movie stuff, just as the gun was. Whoever had sawn its barrels had not taken much pride in his work. He could see that from where he sat.

"You got a licence for that? They're very tough about such things I hear these days."

"How would you like to be scraped off that far wall like strawberry jam?"

"Did anyone ever tell you, Terry, you've got a food-fixation?"

"And you talk like a fucking book."

"But how would *you* know?" Stalemate. They were like two youngsters who had run out of insults. A clock ticked briskly somewhere: on the mantelpiece in the parlour across the hall, the prisoner would have guessed. Outside in the streets a dog barked, children's voices followed, then the source of all their excitement, an ice-cream van sounded its chimes, the first few bars of "Greensleeves". That was something novel to a man so long locked up.

Young Terry saw him smiling to himself and jerked the gun, but he would do nothing until he heard that first click, the man in the chair had decided. And it was surprising how cool he was, considering. But then perhaps after all he welcomed the turn events were taking. When he heard the hammer go back, that's when he would make his move, trusting to instinct to make the right decision for him. But then the sinister little kiss of the mechanism did sound, and he found he was paralysed. It was a shock. He was looking into both barrels and couldn't move. His miscalculation had been immense. Mixed up in his head was an image of that rushing black charge and which vent it might come exploding at him from first – but also there was his own anger at himself. To finish up in some woman's armchair with a newspaper across your lap ... there was nothing so pathetic or tawdry. Should he close his eyes? He was such a sham. He deserved everything.

Then he heard Young Terry whisper, "What's that?" The doctored shotgun drooped. "Did you hear it?"

He was listening intently. From the angle of his head, it was clear he suspected some presence outside the front door. On tiptoes he advanced to the centre of the room, where he stood now like a terrified, overgrown child. The weapon in his hand had, in a moment, indeed become a toy. "For Christ's sake!" The prisoner realised with some shock that the appeal was directed at him.

"Is there somebody at the door?" he heard himself ask stupidly.

"Sssh!" hissed Young Terry. "They'll hear you!"

"Who?"

"Somebody put a key in the lock. Are you deaf?"

He almost said, I thought it was you, but checked himself. But then, as though the unspoken had triggered off what he most dreaded, Young Terry did indeed raise the gun, pulling back both hammers with a single sudden and *noiseless* action. The prisoner thought of the returning churchgoer getting the full blast through her own front door and he half rose from his chair. "Don't! Don't do it, Terry!"

A second later an echo, it seemed, came from the scullery. "No. Don't do it, Terry."

They both gasped. Terry wheeled, the gun tilted – thank god – ceilingwards, and the prisoner, whose view was blocked, heard him cry out, "Galloway, for god's sake!"

The short figure in the scuffed leather aviator's jacket stood between the jambs, calmly chewing. While they watched, still

88

shaken, he hooked out his gum between finger and thumb and rolled it into a hard, dry pellet, then flicked it deftly into the woman's empty grate. They heard it make contact, then, "How did you get in?" whispered Terry. He seemed to have lost his voice.

"Through that wee window back there, and I'm annoyed about it. This key I've got isn't much use when you put the snib across on the front door. Contrary to your orders, you disgusting person, you. Now, hand me over that pea-shooter." He held out his small nicotine-stained hand. Young Terry looked at it as though it were venomous. He licked his lips. "Wooden end first, if you don't mind." The weapon changed hands and instantly Galloway had broken it and was fishing out two bright red cartridges. They went into the pocket of his flying-jacket. The prisoner felt suddenly sick. He let his head loll against the back of his chair and closed his eyes.

"Make the big man here a cup of tea," Galloway ordered, and in a few seconds the electric kettle was humming in the scullery. "No sugar." The prisoner opened his eyes. Galloway was sitting at the table watching him. "No sugar." He said it again in a soft voice, so that only the two of them could hear. They looked at one another. Galloway grinned. Then he went over to the woman's television set and switched it on.

Young Terry came into the room holding a full mug in his massive mitt. He wiped away a drip with a corner of his T-shirt. *Southern Comfort*, it proclaimed in faded brown script, but the prisoner was in no mood for irony. He felt bruised mentally. The buffeting when it came arrived without warning. He would never be able to cope in this mad world, he told himself, or with these mad people, for wasn't it a sign of their insanity that they had adapted themselves to the sudden see-sawings of violence? Some even embraced the idea of it avidly, like this deadly young weasel hunched in the opposite chair. He had a sneer on his face for everyone and everything, including the worshippers on the screen. The sound of hymn-singing now filled the room, coming from a kirk somewhere in his own country.

"Look at them," he announced. "All those tight-arsed hypocrites in their Sunday suits. I'd love to spray a few rounds in among that crew, I can tell you. Just to hear them squeal. And have it televised. Live coverage." Young Terry laughed out loud in the scullery. "He thinks I'm joking!" cried Galloway. "The fat boy in there, he thinks I'm joking! Isn't that right, fat boy?"

"Don't call me that!"

"I'll call you whatever I please, you useless, horrible thing you! Get on with your housework!" He glanced across. "More tea?" The prisoner shook his head. He was trying to remember what he had been like himself at that age. A gun hadn't been far from his hand either, but he had been licensed to kill by Her Majesty's Britannic Government, culling treacherous wogs in the swamps and paddies of Malaya. And it was enjoyable, that part of it, no point in pretending otherwise. It stayed with you a long time afterwards. Something about the way this one talked reminded him of that feeling, the contempt for civilians and their fat, safe lives, the knowledge gained and never to be forgotten of how easy it would be to snuff out anyone at any given time or place. The dangerous little rodent in the other chair was watching him, as though he could read his thoughts, smiling at him. Perhaps he was conscious of an affinity as well. The prisoner had already noted his tattoos.

Then the programme changed on the television screen and a newsreader's voice was heard intoning over film of a street in some far Fermanagh town. A butcher's shop-front stayed in shot while the details of the latest atrocity were read out. The owner had been discovered in his fridge that very morning, hung on a hook like one of his own carcases. A neighbour had made the discovery after hearing a car drive off in the early hours. He retold his story for the viewers who could now see how he furnished his home. In this other kitchen, sixty miles away, the three of them looked into someone else's living quarters and thought nothing of it. The man in his chair spoke directly to them, but the words had little or no impact. It wasn't distance that robbed his testimony of horror, but merely its rehearsed rise and fall. And in a moment the newsreader would be smiling and leaving them with an item on the newest addition to London Zoo . . .

But before he got to the pandas there was a final item on the home front. Soundlessly a face filled the screen and was held there. The prisoner looked into his own eyes, fixed by the camera shutter on a day ten years earlier. It was the photograph they always used of him, taken on the day his sentence had begun. He heard the others in the room draw in breath incredulously before he had time to feel any emotion, then the picture had melted to one – a living one, this time – of a weary-looking pensioner doing his best to avoid facing into the camera.

"Tell me, Mr Steele," the eager young reporter was saying "your son . . ." The old man twisted as though already skewered on the thrusting microphone. He was wearing an old jacket which the prisoner felt he recognised, one of his own cast-offs with its fifties lapels and patch pockets. It dwarfed him, made him look ridiculous, much as he himself looked now. Someone should be made to pay for all this humiliation to a family, the prisoner told himself. His hands gripped the wooden arms of his chair as he listened to what this interviewing youth was saying about him. "He's now seriously ill, the doctors tell us, he must have treatment for his condition, and that the longer he delays the greater the risk will be . . . What do you say to that, Mr Steele?" The old man standing on his own doorstep wriggled even more painfully. Then, swallowing, "I think the doctors are wrong," and closed the front door on the reporter and the great viewing public.

Galloway hooted with glee, beating the side of his chair with an open palm. "Good for you, pop!" but the prisoner knew there was nothing to crow about. He felt pain for the old man and his shame. He felt for himself even more deeply in a surge of self-pity, for it seemed to him that he had just witnessed the final act of his own betrayal.

Then Young Terry moved his great bulk over to the television and turned it off. His face was mottled and angry. "Billy said he wasn't to watch the news. You should know better, Ned Galloway."

The picture diminished to a bright searing dot. Seated in their chairs, they watched it intently as though nothing had occurred and, sure enough, Galloway said, "I'll pretend that didn't happen," and then, "but when I've counted up to ten I'll expect to be watching a picture again."

Terry attempted a brave laugh from the depths of the scullery. They also heard him mutter something defiant above the clatter of the dishes. Galloway rose almost casually from his chair. He looked reasonable, prepared to reason, as he went into the little back room. Then Young Terry screamed out, at first in disbelief, then in agony. Something broke in pieces on the floor and was ground underfoot. Trembling in his chair, the prisoner kept his eyes fixed on the grey screen, but his hearing made him a participant in whatever horror had erupted in there among the mops and the pails. Sobbing broke out now, from the huddled bulk on the floor. He could hear Galloway stepping over the other where he lay. Galloway came back into the kitchen looking no different and dropped into his chair, where, coolly, he raised a shoe to pick off a small embedded fragment of white china. He examined it carefully for a moment, then he flicked it at the dead screen.

"Time to make tracks," he announced.

Automatically the prisoner stood up. The two of them made a strange pair on their feet together in that woman's kitchen, the ferret and the tired rabbit, a good head-and-a-half in height between them. Still, if it ever came to a showdown there was little doubt in the rabbit's mind as to which would prevail, even though knowledge of most of the other's fighting tricks might even the score somewhat.

Terry was groaning now, oblivious to everything save the pain between his legs. It seemed he was to be left lying there like that, but, at the door, Galloway turned and came back one last time to the scullery. His voice was quiet, reasonable. "You got that, not because of your bad manners, but because I don't like people messing about with what doesn't concern them. Our friend here is *my* concern. While he's in *my* care, no one gives him any aggro. Get that? I hope you do, because next time, if there is a next time, I'll do more than just damage your marriage prospects for you – fat boy."

Outside in the street, the air was almost heady after the human fog he had just left. He staggered a little and felt the other's hand on his arm, then was steered towards a car, a solitary and empty blue saloon parked in the distance. He blinked rapidly, trying to clear his mind of the haze which seemed somehow to have entered it.

His imagination had constructed an ordered scene of Sunday peace, a neat terrace of houses, each with a coat of fresh paintwork and a concave step scrubbed as a matter of habit. He knew such streets well; nothing had dimmed their image from the past. They existed out there reassuringly, whenever he had cared to think about them in that other alien world of wire mesh and dog patrols. But this was the true terrain of nightmare, fixed in its horrible aftermath. A vista of bricked-up doorways and windows stretched for as far as the eye could travel, for it was one of those immensely long, slightly curving streets, artery for all those little side streets which, together on the map, went to make up a defined city-area with its own nickname and loyalties. But all that was dead and done, merely a memory now. They picked their way through sodden debris and drifts of wind-blown rubbish, past the brutal breeze-block facings in the older brick. There was a reek of soot, damp and escaping gas. The pressure on his elbow never ceased once. The prisoner reflected that this fierce little runt guiding him must be drawn to such places, remembering the car-breaker's site and its identical air of desolation. On somebody's house wall an aerosol had lately been at work on the new concrete. The prisoner saw his name in brutal black script. *Silver Lives.*

"Home sweet home, eh, big man?" murmured his escort, smiling crookedly.

He had produced a bunch of car keys from the recesses of his flying jacket. Three of them went into the lock before he was lucky, then they were inside sitting in the fug of another strange car. A plastic madonna was fixed to the dashboard. They both looked at it, then exchanged glances, and the little man was still laughing at the joke as he pulled out and away from the kerb.

He began talking almost at once, as though needing to confide in someone. "This scene is getting to be not on, you know what I mean? Cowboys all over the shop. I mean, I don't mind taking risks, but with some of these rodeo stars, you're taking your life in your hands. You know what I mean, man?" Deftly he brought out his old tobacco tin and pressed open its lid without taking his other hand from the wheel. "Have a puff. Go on, it'll relax you."

The prisoner took one of the rolled cigarettes. "I don't smoke."

The other laughed. "Live dangerously." He laughed again as the first herbal fumes began to fill the car.

Outside, the ravaged houses still sped past, although here and there the prisoner noticed signs of habitation, a door, a window still curtained. He must have spent the night in one such outpost, he told himself, oblivious of the rats and the creeping rot behind the bedroom wallpaper.

"Pretty, isn't it?" He felt as though his thoughts had been on display.

"It reminds me of the Blitz." And it did, except for the absence of people. The streets seemed always crowded then as though there was an impatience to rebuild. But this territory had been abandoned for good, nothing seemed surer.

"I didn't know you had that here."

"Oh, yes, we had ours too."

"They must have kept the Gorbals the way Hitler left it then."
It was something shared. The feeling made the prisoner
uneasy. The unrelenting antagonism he had come to expect
seemed to him much more preferable somehow.

"Anyway, I won't have to look at it much longer. As soon as I get
my seaman's ticket, I'm off to Rio." He hummed a fragment of
something Latin. His passenger wondered if it wasn't perhaps
the influence of the weed. He had felt nothing himself so far.

"You can get one, you know, for a couple of hundred, down at
the docks. If you have the right contacts. Nae bother. And then,
South America take it away." There was something forced
about all this. "It's the only life. You just pick the fruit off the
trees." Then, winking, he added, "*You* should try it, big man,"
and throwing back his head, he guffawed loudly at what he saw as
a joke.

The prisoner wondered how such a delusion could ever have
taken hold, that nothing more than a suntan could change so
much. He remembered other men like this one, from the same
city, with the same instincts. The poison-dwarfs, they had been
nicknamed, with their blades sewn lovingly into the peaks of their
bonnets. There had been a regiment of them here in this very
town, until they were posted elsewhere because of the outcry. His
distaste fastened on the visible, the narrow shoulders, the
outlines of each skinny thigh in denim, the hands on the steering-
wheel with their ginger hairs and the tattooed initials across the
freckled span of fingers. A.C.A.B. All Coppers Are Bastards.

They had passed out of the wasteland by this time into a
neighbourhood where people occasionally strolled and children
played on street-corners, but there still seemed nothing settled
or solid about it. At any moment, the big man decided, all of this
could slide effortlessly back into decay, and he would be back
once more amongst those burnt-out shells given over only to
vermin. The word clung uncomfortably. He was riding in the
same car as something of the species right at this moment, he told
himself. He moved over in his seat, but the other didn't seem to
notice. He was still embroidering a tropical fantasy as he drove,
the smoke trickling from his nostrils.

"Copacabana . . . That Ronald Biggs was no dozer, was he? Eh?
He could have went anywhere, so he could, couldn't he? But

where does he land up? Eh? I'll run into him. Bound to. Put it there, Ronnie, baby. Meet a number one fan ..."

The car was about to reach an intersection and, as its gears shuddered gently in readiness, the prisoner, pressed up against the door, felt something hard dig into his side. His hand met a lever and, to his astonishment, it gave under his touch. Cold air flowed about him. He sat staring straight ahead, wondering how long it would be before the man at his side noticed. It didn't occur to him to take advantage of his discovery. Later he was to marvel at that, at how docile an animal he had become but here, now, he simply waited to be told to shut the door.

Then Galloway *did* swear loudly, but it wasn't on account of the sudden draught. Ahead of them another car had pulled out unexpectedly from the kerb, and they both fastened their attention on the flushed, bald head of its driver. "You stupid.. .!" Then the man's old Hillman stalled and Galloway stamped on the brake, shouting obscenities. Their own car filled with fresh air as the passenger-door swung wide, and the prisoner felt himself falling. Galloway's face had a look of dumb amazement on it, then his mouth opened to yell something.

It was that and, with it, anticipation of the sound the other's voice would make, that forced the prisoner to his feet. His palms burned – they had taken the force of his tumble on the gritty road. He brushed them quickly, automatically, against his trouser legs then, still trembling, he started to run. Behind him the car engine roared on and on, like some thwarted animal. As he ran up the alley-way with his hands over his ears.

11

WHEN THE PHONE RANG the first time, she stirred sluggishly in her sleep, then tried to blot out the sound by sliding down deeper beneath the bedclothes. But it burred away beyond the layers of duck-down and cotton with all the persistence of its tribe.

Nan groaned. One bare arm left the nest, bumped against something in the darkness; she heard her watch fall to the floor. She couldn't remember having asked for an alarm-call, yet it was certainly that sort of time, she didn't have to be told, when one heard the operator's flat tones reminding that there was a plane to catch in the grey morning hours. But she had no plans of that sort, at least not just yet. Her groping hand found, then pulled the receiver off the hook. She lay there and waited for the expected ache in her temples to take possession. She tried not to think of how much she had got through on her own last night. Dead soldiers, where they lay on the carpet, behind the settee, beneath the coffee table, to remind her later.

There was a woman in one of the other flats, unmarried or

divorced, in her fifties, and going to seed, if that was the expression, seedy, certainly, and once she had heard the clink of her empties in her shopping-bag. The woman had blushed, lowering her head as she hurried past. She wondered where she dumped all her little quarter-bottles; she favoured the handbag-size herself. When she got on that plane, Nan hoped that reminders of that sort would be left behind for good, but then, to be realistic, London was hardly the place for that, was it? The secret sisterhood of those who tippled on the sly was surely greater there. Bed-sitter and the nightly trip to the off-licence awaited her, she had no illusions on that score, but even that was one step up from the life she now lived. And, she told herself, if you started off without illusions then you couldn't be disappointed. She was no longer the young hopeful trembling on the brink of a new life.

As though to remind herself, she sent her hands on an exploratory run along her body under the bedclothes. The comfortably rounded, but still firm belly – it had never known a corset – the solid flanks, thighs, and, where they converged, that still spreading bush. None of that was the mark of someone green and unripe. Autumn was her season. Cupping her heavy breasts, she felt a tickle of desire. Men there certainly would be, there always had been, and she knew that most of them would still be married. But this time there might be the occasional one who was different, to break that long chain, with their parked cars and their children's toys, always small enough to remain hidden under the back seat, until she felt them biting up into her as though out of family spite. She could have had her own vicious little menagerie of souvenirs, if she had wished.

When they asked her if she lived alone – and they always did, sooner or later – she would lie and say she shared with two other girls. It was funny how she almost got to know those non-existent flatmates, re-inventing them and their little ways each time. One *would* hang her dripping tights over the bath, just when you wanted to use it. The other was the quiet, plain one, who rarely went out, and thus the most useful, from that point of view. Sometimes she even became a Sunday School teacher with strong Presbyterian principles. They were part of her private life, two ghosts inhabiting the same two rooms, kitchen and bath, she paid so handsomely for. She needed them, just as she needed the protection of her front door, after she had put all its bolts across and settled down with the first stiff vodka of the evening. Lying in the dark and listening to her blood beat, the details of the room and the other rooms beyond were imprinted on her inner eye – a door there, a mirror, a wardrobe, a table there – or so she told herself.

She had still knocked her watch to the floor. Now her trailing hand dredged it up from the carpet, held it close to her face, but the luminous dial refused to sharpen into focus. She jiggled the phone until the line was clear, then dialled the speaking-clock. ". . . five forty-two and twenty seconds," enunciated the middle-class lady somewhere in the Home Counties.

Without thinking, Nan put back the receiver, and immediately the thing rang. It rang with a new and vicious note, or so it seemed to her, and this time she knew there was to be no escape from its petulance. She snapped on the bedside lamp and stared at it. Then she lifted the handset and put it to her ear, but not too close. At first she thought she had got herself a heavy breather, like that other one who used to pester her until she bought herself a whistle, but there were no whispered obscenities this time. Not yet.

The man's voice spoke her name hesitantly, and somehow that was much worse. "Nan?"

She sat up in bed listening. "Who is it?" Then, "How did you get my number?" almost hysterically, for that was what terrified most, the combining of name and private number, deadly information in this city at this time.

There was a pause as though he were thinking about answering, then he said, "It's me. Silver. Silver Steele," but she still couldn't get the other thing out of her head.

"Who gave you this number? *Who?*"

"I need your help, Nan. I rang earlier."

"*Who?*"

She heard him sigh. "It was on the back of that card you gave me. You must have –"

"Do you know what time it is? It's a quarter to six!"

"I haven't a watch. For god's sake, this is my last tuppence. Don't let it run out!"

She asked, "Where are you?" knowing full well the penalty for getting involved with this penniless man without a watch. Those were the sort of details that swayed her, soft, giddy bitch that she was.

Now he hesitated on the other end of the line in his call-box, and she knew what he was thinking. "Don't worry," she said. "I won't shop you."

She heard him taking strength from her voice. "The Botanic Gardens. There's a school . . . in a quiet street," coming in a rush.

"I know it," she said. "I'll be there in about twenty minutes. My car is a blue Beetle."

"Beetle? What's that?" He sounded panic-stricken.

"You'll know when you see it. And hear it."

She put down the receiver and hugged her bare knees, sitting up in the now disordered bed, as though the last minutes had been particularly energetic ones. But the struggle had all been in her head. She was left with the dying echoes as she stared straight ahead of her at her old Bogart poster. Every morning she awoke to that tight-lipped stoicism, just the two of them knowing the soft centre beneath the dangerous exterior. Silver, she thought . . . Silver Steele. A name from any one of a dozen old movies. The resemblance was laughable.

Wearily she rose from the sheets and padded into the small kitchen, not bothering to put on a dressing-gown – a bonus for any window-cleaner. Not that she cared, for her mouth felt gritty while the rest of her was in keeping with that sensation of having been a receptacle for almost anything and everything the night before. While her kettle boiled, she thought of what she had promised just a moment ago. She felt committed, even though she could easily put the phone-call down to a bad dream. The memory of a nightmare always faded in time; why not just go back to bed for the rest of the day? She stirred her coffee, watching the granules of powdered milk sink and dissolve. The first sip scalded, yet she thought of him, coffeeless, comfortless, shivering in a phone-box, at the park. Why there? Had he spent the night in the open? His suit was thin, the cheapest there was. Her own skin prickled at the thought.

"Oh, fuck it!" she cried out. "And him!"

She flung the rest of her coffee into the sink and went back into the bedroom. Under the duvet she lay with her knees to her chin, trying to put that haggard countenance out of mind. In the heating darkness there should have been only room for her and her concerns alone, yet it seemed as though he were there too. Her imagination insisted that if she stretched out her hand only a little way it would encounter that bony frame. She had touched it already, that had been her mistake. The covers were now stifling; she flung them off and lay staring at the ceiling.

In the flat above, the first movements of the day would soon begin. Groans, then furniture being bumped, a cistern flushing, taps running, the radio – all leading to the final slam of the door, then silence. All over the house, the same ritual would take its course, until the place was empty, save for her still in her bed. She could tell they resented her, all those yawning workers as they passed her nameplate, even her fellow-tippler with the plaid holdall. Today was Monday; it would be worse than usual. She could almost anticipate the bad temper once it began seeping down to her.

The house was old. Once it had been inhabited by a single well-to-do family and its servants. Then the continuity had been broken for good with its conversion into "flats" – some were mere hutches under the eaves, where the skivvies used to sleep. There were twelve bell-pushes now beside the front door. Outwardly the villa looked unchanged, red brick, sandstone facings, set generously back from the road behind glossy rhododendrons, but those tiny white and luminous buttons, each with its owner's name beside it in smudged script, gave the game away. They always reminded her of what a cold, unnatural home life they all had of it, each in their tiny partitioned-off existence, listening to one another's coughs and creaks. She thought of the terraced house in which she had been born, the street, the neighbours and their neighbourliness. That had come to be cloying eventually, but now she mourned the passing of all those comings and goings. The man in the phone booth had come from a street like hers. At the time of his trial she had noted its name, and its locality, a rougher one than hers, certainly, but that meant nothing to her any longer. Nan mourned a time when everyone she knew went home in the evening to a small kitchen-house where the fire in the range never went out, winter or summer. Children were bathed on Saturday nights before its glow, in a bath that hung down from a nail in the coal-house the rest of the week. People washed themselves at a thick brown sink in the scullery; the water closet was out in the yard. Her father would say, "Ten o'clock, my girl, no later, or the door will be locked," and she would rush out to put on lipstick before the mirror in the phone box. Four girls jostling, giggling and sharing the same tube of Lucky Pink.

Someone above her head groaned long and loudly. The sound

seemed to symbolise everything that was wrong with her life. This house was peopled with sleep-walkers, she told herself. Soon they would start stumbling past her own door and out into the streets of the city to join all the other robots. No, she couldn't face another winter of it, not here in this bleak, black outpost, where the rain buckled the plywood fronts of the shops, while, before their doors, the pot-holes filled steadily, where the bus windows never seemed to get washed except by more rain, where hands pawed you at the security-checks, and the bars were full of roaring, unhappy drunks. More and more she seemed to be in a frontier town, the men in stained parkas with rabbitskin ruffs, hauling themselves in and out of cars which, like their owners, looked expendable. No, she wanted the grime of this Murmansk of a place scrubbed off for good – just as soon as she could stretch out in a London bathtub.

She looked at her watch. The hands swept on remorselessly. Already she was late for her rendezvous, that is, if she meant to keep it. Did she? She certainly knew one thing, she couldn't lie here a minute longer listening to the dawn chorus from upstairs. Before she left the place for good, she must telephone a bomb-scare to one of the other flats, just to hear the news travel and watch the commotion. She felt she had a lot of revenge left in her, not just for them and all the other burghers, but for the city itself. It had cheated her, by changing from the innocent slip of a young thing she thought of it as being once upon a time – her time – to the ugly old whore it now was.

A dangerous line of thought, she said to herself, laughing at her reflection in the bathroom mirror. She didn't bother with make-up, just a dab of talcum powder in the strategic places. She pulled on her velour top over bare skin, jeans, flat shoes. No one would recognise her as the same fashion plate who normally stepped out around noon in an aura of Arpège.

At the door she took a last look at Sam Spade. The eyes followed her – a photographer's trick, she'd heard somewhere. She could almost read his thoughts, "How dumb can a broad get," as she closed the door on her own particular brand of disorder.

12

HE HAD SPENT THE NIGHT under glass, in the vast and domed, tropical plant house, he and all the other prize specimens.

After the park gates had been padlocked, the sound drifted across the green spaces to where he hunkered in the bushes, four distinct detonations in all; not until then did he dare go prowling. He should have felt a lifting of the spirits at having all of this to himself, but he continued to run crouching from cover to cover for a long time, until he fetched up by the Victorian greenhouse. One of its ventilators was open, and, after a moment's hesitation, he climbed inside.

And so, until dawn, he was back once more in the steam heat of Malayan jungles. He recognised the humidity and the plant odours immediately. Soon the thin fabric of his jacket was clinging to his back. He peeled it off and, gradually, the rest of what he was wearing, until a gaunt white man, naked save for a pair of garish jockey-pants, was padding restlessly up and down the narrow aisles between the hanging foliage. Sleep was out of the question in that temperature, but the thought of a night in the open, curled up on a bench, made him count his blessings. To pass the time, he read the Latin names on the wooden markers, until it was too dark to make them out. He wondered if any of the plants were edible; nothing had passed his lips since morning. Like a hen under a hedge, he kept changing nests until something he'd read once about plants at night discharging carbon dioxide – or was it the other way round? – made him settle beneath the open ventilator. His discarded clothes made a thin layer on the gravel; he sat cross-legged, watching darkness gather, while his sweat trickled. It seemed an impossibility that there was any fat left on him to render down.

Up until then he had given little or no real thought to what he was going to do. Since he had tumbled out of the car, all his reflexes had been automatic and unthinking, like those of any hunted animal. His legs carried him until they felt weak, then he came to a place where he could ease them. It was only when he had dropped on to the park bench that it came to him how perfect a place he had settled upon, where tramps and derelicts barely receive a glance. By some intuition he had hit on the only class among whom he could lose himself. Surreptitiously he tried to make his clothes even more offhand; he pulled off a button or two, he manhandled the already wrinkled fabric, but the rest of the down and outs, the Woodpecker drinkers, weren't fooled, even if the strolling citizenry seemed to be. He saw the winos watching him out of bleary eyes as they huddled on their benches passing their brown bottles to and fro.

Finally he got up and walked into the tropical fish house, where he pretended interest in the goldfish. In a foot of tepid water, they slid below over a softly moving carpet of breadcrumbs and sweet wrappers. He stayed there until three youths he noticed were staring at him. It made him uneasy, although later he was to discover that everyone did that these days, as though trusting by some effort of will to read the bomber's intention in his face. He moved quickly out into the dying afternoon sun, seeking the loneliest paths he could find.

Now he was alone and squatting in his jungle, only a strangely silent one, the great glossy leaves on their stalks all around inching imperceptibly upwards to an invisible dome. A reddish glimmer filtered through from the city's lights. It coated his limbs, made them appear healthier than they were, than he felt.

103

Sweat gleamed. He remembered how he had sweltered on the massage table, that girl, her sympathy. She had put something in his pocket: a card. He felt about in the damp folds of his jacket until he found it, then moved it this way and that, trying to read what meaning, if any, it might hold for him. He rose from his nest in a search for better light, holding the thin pasteboard close to the glass, but still it remained only a pale blur.

And so he remained, trying not to pin too much hope on the little pink rectangle now lying before him on the gravel, waiting for first light. He dared not handle it further nor even put it back in his breast pocket for fear any pencilled writing it held might be smudged. At the same time the action was rational, yet irrational, but it was more and more the way his mind was working. He must not get too obsessive, he told himself, no matter how desperate his plight seemed.

Dawn came, or rather, one rosy glow cancelled out the other artificial one, then grew stronger until, with nervous fingers, he took the card up again. *Bebe's*, he read, *For The Best Massage In Town. Our Business, Your Pleasure. Thank You. Come Again.* And underneath, a phone number. He turned the card over. His heart beat, there was another number, handwritten in biro. It was his lucky combination, he felt certain of it. The more he studied the digits, memorised them, even added them the way he had once done as a child, with tram tickets, hoping for magic, the more they became his and his alone. It seemed unthinkable that, dialled, they would evoke a stranger's voice.

He shivered and, in that moment, recognised reality. He rose to his feet and, staggering a little with dizziness and cramp, began to pull on his clinging duds. If this pain in his head didn't finish him off, he told himself grimly, then the chill he was going to catch certainly would.

He crawled out of his jungle refuge into the autumn morning, surprised to see the first faint signs of frost. Now he did shiver and with a vengeance. He began to run on the path to keep up circulation, but also for fear of leaving his spoor on the grass. It was all silver and pristine, like the first day of creation, every spider's web outlined for all the world to see, but he was the only one abroad.

He ran all the way to the far gate. Beyond, he knew, there was a coin box. The name should have halted him in his tracks, long before he reached the railings and climbed up over, for his pockets were empty, but all he could think of were the numbers he kept repeating to himself as he ran. Seven, three, one, *four*, oh, oh. Already they had acquired their own rhythm which couldn't be altered.

Without hesitating, he dialled, then waited for the miracle. The ringing tones stretched out across the sleeping city, sounding in a room he couldn't imagine. Then abruptly, the pulse changed to something steady and high-pitched. For the first time he became aware of where he was, what he was doing. He stared at the cold black receiver humming in his hand, at the slots beneath for the coins. He clapped his pockets remembering, then, defeated, put the phone slowly back on its cradle. Leaning against the glass, he closed his eyes; why not let this place be the end of the road for him? Just dial *them* – *they* were always awake – and within minutes a car would be outside. He thought, with irony, and no money needed either, for the number was printed beside the mirror boldly like an invitation. All his problems solved at a stroke, this pain in his head put right, food, clothes, his own bed again, a return to the way it used to be. Why not? Why hadn't he done it earlier? He had, after all, only to walk up to the nearest man in a uniform ...

He stared at his face in the mirror. It didn't belong. Not here. Even the dossers in the park had twigged that. He looked away from his reflection – why do they put mirrors in telephone boxes? – and out through the smudged glass. Beyond in the park he could see a mound, its outline, even at this late season, still obscured by growing things, their colour predominantly tawny, but, in the heart of it all, something scarlet. The plant, whatever it was, seemed to burn, drawing his eyes like flame. He could appreciate that, even if he had been born in a slum, thinking of geraniums put out on window sills to drink in the sooty rain. No, he wouldn't give all this up just yet. He might still be able to move freely about a little longer. The old magic in the tram tickets might still hold good for him. Seven, three, one, *four*, oh, oh.

He pushed out of the phone box, lips mouthing, then up and over the railings again to drop back into the park. He began to run again. He remembered where he had seen coins: lying on the floor of the goldfish pond, flung there by the youths who, tiring of the sport, had then turned their attention on him.

13

"THE GIANT'S RING," she said, in answer to his question. "Don't tell me you haven't heard of it."

They were sitting in her Volkswagen with the engine cooling. Under the wheels, a grassy track led straight to the heart of the old earthworks. The place had a spooky reputation on certain dates in the calendar, but on almost every other night of the year it was better known for a different reason. Nose to bumper, parked cars stretched back all the way to the main road, windows steamed up, with only an occasional lighted match to betray the fact that there might be life inside. Then, as though at some pre-arranged signal, the last car to arrive would reverse out slowly to set the rest in motion, a lovers' convoy with discreetly dipped lights to preserve anonymity.

"Mind you, there's not so much of it these nights," she said, thinking aloud. "Not if you don't want to end up like something on a butcher's slab."

He looked at her. "What some of your friends like to do for

kicks?" Oh, he knew all right; it was in his face.

"You have some funny ideas about me – and then to help me like this."

"It's not every day I get the chance to rub shoulders with a celebrity." *Oh, your big mouth, girl.*

"Elbows," he said, looking down. "That song. You know, rubbing elbows at the Ritz . . .?"

"You're cracked," she said.

"I wouldn't doubt it for a minute."

She laughed. "You need a wash."

"Badly?"

She opened a window, and they both laughed. "I'm sorry," she said.

A bird was singing quite close. "A lark," he said. "You get a lot of them out by the Motorway for some reason."

She thought of the towers and the high mesh fences – she hadn't before – as she raced past in her car, seeing them as just outlines in the distance. A place to read about in the newspapers, a place as remote from her own concerns as Siberia. "They're on strike at the moment. Did you know that ? Extra privileges or something."

"So they went ahead with it," he said.

"Would you have been involved? If you'd been still . . . inside." She hesitated on the last word. It sounded like something from a bad film.

His face showed nothing. "We have to keep in the public eye. People's memories are short. All governments trade on that."

"Mao Tse-tung has spoken."

For a moment, she thought, he's going to get angry this time. Instead he sighed, spreading his hands on his lap. She noticed how well-kept they still were. "Women believe . . ." He stopped.

"Oh, Christ!" She rolled down the window savagely, leaning her head on the sill.

". . . in forcing issues. Don't they? Don't *you*? You think I'm cold."

"As a fucking fish!"

"A *bull* is a stupid animal too. He has a ring in his nose."

She turned on him. "What makes you such a bloody intellectual? Superior. You're not, you know. You're from the same wee street, just like all the rest of us."

"A German once said the Irish always reminded him of a pack

107

of hounds pulling down a stag, but, Nan, we only drag down our own kind. Or try to."

"I bet you'd never say things like that if you were back in *that* place."

Again he sighed. "You people. The newspapers and the television do all your thinking for you. But then I suppose it's easier to believe it's all like some prison picture you've seen. All that drama. Believe me, there's not much of that. Killing time, not each other, is the big problem. And the smell. But then, you don't get that in a movie, do you? Sweat, disinfectant, bad feet. And the boiled cabbage. One of the reasons for the present protest, if I remember."

It was a big speech coming from him. His face had gone grey again, as if it had taken a lot out of him. She felt compassion, but at the same time something perverse made her want to go on digging deeper. She had earned the right.

"Freedom fighters!" she sneered. "Who do you lot think you're kidding?" He didn't say a thing. "Go on, convince me. You've got this great reputation. I've read some of your interviews."

She laid her hand on his thigh. It was not the mocking gesture he must have taken it for; he pulled his leg away. Leaning back against her door and facing him squarely, she said, "Am I giving you a bad time?" All right, damn it, she *was* forcing the issue.

A flicker of a smile came to his pale lips. "Girls in cars parked here usually give a man a *good* time, don't they?"

"At seven in the morning?"

"I'm sorry about that. I'd no one else to turn to. My last shot . . . in the dark."

She said, "You can say that again," shivering. She had never been here before in daylight. It all looked smaller than she'd imagined it to be, not the great, brooding Stonehenge of a place that came to mind. Fresh cow-droppings marked the grass; there were blackberries on a bush a foot away from the open window. She put her hand out to pick the ripest. "So you *have* been here before, in your youth," she said, munching.

"No, you hear the men talking."

"About girls?"

"Not too much of that."

"They say you run the place like a monastery."

"You shouldn't believe everything you read in the papers. Journalists either lie or exaggerate. I think I blame them almost as much as I do politicians. For what's happened."

It suddenly struck her how privileged she was to be sitting here like this with the most wanted man in her part of the island. "Some of those journalists you mention would pay a packet for what you're telling me."

"They would, and then they'd twist it around to fit the politics of their paper."

"One last question – for the women readers." He was looking at her mouth. The blackberry stain, she thought. "What do you do about . . . sex? In that place?"

"About sex?"

"Yes."

With a straight face he said, "We usually have our tea then."

She made a grab for him. She'd wanted to for a long time, an odd compulsion surely, a return to school and the same yen all the girls seemed to share for one boy in particular, tall and staid, with spectacles, more than a bit self-contained, like this one. The breath left him in a rush – she was a hefty girl – he raised his knee to defend himself. "I knew you had tickles," she panted.

"*Christalmighty, have you gone mad?*"

She kept on at him all the same, just like a terrier. Maybe I have – a bit, she thought. "Please, please," he protested. "You don't know your own strength."

She wanted to laugh now – the words, his face, the situation. "Okay," she said. He still kept his knee up. "Give in?"

"Yes, yes," he said. They watched each other warily. "Are all the women like this nowadays?"

"Too true, buster. We take what we want."

"Good god," he groaned. "I should have stayed where I was."

She could see he had entered into the spirit of things – at least, a little. She became softer, more seductive. "We have some unfinished business." I am a right slut, she thought, and no mistake.

"I don't think I'm up to it," he said.

"Use your memory, big boy." She had a sudden image: old Sam raising his eyes heavenwards. "Did anyone ever tell you you look a bit like Humphrey Bogart? You're taller, of course. He was only five foot ten, but you'd never know that, from the screen. They had to put Alan Ladd on a box for some of *his* scenes. Funny, isn't it, how small they all are, Dustin Hoffman, Paul Newman . . ."

It was like a scene in a dentist's, him in the chair staring straight ahead, trying not to think of what was happening to him. She touched a sensitive spot. "So, there is life! Who would have thought it?"

"Nan –" he began.

"You're quite right," she said briskly, "let's get into the back."

She swung her legs out, felt them showered with dew from her bramble bush. The wet pierced like needles. There was mist too, a loose grey perimeter hemming them in. He was still sitting in the car. Maybe the poor bugger does believe all of us have gone cock-crazy, she thought. What a laugh. She felt dangerously light-headed, looking around her as though this were to be her last glimpse of native soil. Good riddance, she thought, you're only fit for pigs anyway.

"Come on," she called out in the still September air, "let's be having you, big boy!" and he emerged dutifully to stand beside the car.

They looked at one another over the domed roof. With her forefinger she traced his name on the sweating metal, casually. It could stay there, she thought, no one would think anything of it. Silver. Already that morning on the way to the park to pick him up she had seen it at least half a dozen times by different hands.

"Cheer up," she said, "I've a surprise for you. When was the last time you were at the seaside?"

14

"SURE YOU'RE ALL RIGHT, SON?" The little man in the outsize duffle coat was leaning forward solicitously. "Doesn't do to mix your drinks. The grain and the grape, you know."

He shuddered slightly as he spoke, glancing down at the diversity of glasses on the table. Their dregs spanned a wide spectrum, from the palest, neat Gordon's, to the ripe plum of a nameless liqueur, for Galloway had reached the stage where now he merely pointed to a bottle behind the bar which caught his eye or his fancy. So far he hadn't been sick though, and no bloody sign of it either . . .

He punished his whisky yet again and the pensioner facing him quickly raised his glass in emulation. "Pardon me for mentioning it, son, but you look as if you've been in the wars."

The man across the table from him merely grunted. The reaction was not unexpected however. Barely a word had come from this wee Scotchie ever since he had entered the pub after the last race at Sandown. Why not join him, he had thought,

111

despite the dried blood, for who would harm an old soldier? "Ach, sure, it's a thankless task keeping the Queen's peace in this town." You could always tell a man who had served, or was serving his country. It was written all over this one. Battle fatigue.

"I got my knock at Tobruk. Monty was good, I grant you, but the Desert Fox was the daddy of them all."

Galloway threw another pound note on to the wet table to shut him up. For a veteran, his drinking companion had remarkably swift reactions. Another time he might have found some amusement in the speed with which his money was snatched and borne to the bar, but his mind seethed with other matters. The drinking and its manner was either a way of fuelling his rage, or dulling it — he still couldn't be sure of the outcome. In the meantime, he would continue pouring the stuff down.

He looked around at the other late-afternoon drinkers. Their faces showed the effects of an overly extended lunch break. There wasn't one of them he couldn't drink under the table, he told himself fiercely. National pride insisted upon it, even if his deep contempt for them did not. He continued to stare, knowing how dangerous that was in this city; but then even to sit in this downtown bar, for him, was an act of recklessness. In the past he had observed the rules. Self-preservation demanded it. Now — from now on — all that had changed. He looked down at his clenched knuckles. They were raw, they throbbed, yet he exulted in the pain, just as he wore the blood on his face with a similar bravado.

His glass was empty. He glared around as though it were *their* fault, all these punters with their heads together over a drink, as if what they were saying to one another was the most momentous thing in the world. He knew different. A business type in a far corner was staring back at him with a startled expression on his red, puffy face. Galloway realised he had been smiling to himself, in itself a disturbing enough sight, but combined with his battle scars . . .

Grandad arrived, bringing with him a whiff of stale tobacco and peppermints. "Your change, son, for what it's worth," he said, spreading the coins delicately in a pool of wet. "Scotch whisky you wanted, wasn't it?"

"Why not? It's mother's milk, isn't it?"

The old man bared his top set, then drank. Emboldened, he ventured, "Tell me, son . . ." but Galloway was thinking of those dentures, pink as fish gills, grinning hideously in a glass of water. Tiny bubbles encrusted them like something marine. He was remembering the tenement in Ogilvy Wynd, his father's hand spilling the tumbler, being made to crawl for them under the bed, their slimy touch . . .

"Where's the bog?" he muttered, lurching to his feet, trying to keep the nausea out of his voice.

In the mirror, a battered flyweight stared back at him. He had no way of telling whether the nose was broken or not. He hoped it was. He was careful to wash only the corner of his mouth where there were traces of vomit. From the tap he drank deeply, but his throat still felt scalded. It would pass, he told himself, just as his face would heal – in time. A matter of time, that was the phrase. Another of those useless expressions. Every time someone opened his mouth back in the bar there, out they dribbled. He didn't have to hear what they were saying to know that. If he had his way it would be rationed, all that meaningless shit about the weather, sport, politics, cars, sex . . .

Behind him the door opened and one of the babblers lurched in, unzipping as he came. He leaned on the veined porcelain with a grunt of relief. "In one end, out the other, eh?" Galloway ignored him. He was dabbing at his knuckles.

"I see old Smokey back there was tapping you for a few drinks," the flushed young executive persisted. "Has he got round to the Afrika Korps yet?"

Galloway stared at him. The other laughed. "You know, Rommel and all that . . ."

Galloway said, "That's my feyther you're talking about, chum," deliberately coarsening the accent.

The other sprayed the trouser legs of his fine Hepworth's suiting. "Christ, Mac, no offence! I had no idea. He's been coming in here for years scroung . . ." going pale at his blunder, even forgetting his damp pinstripes.

Galloway said, "I'm ower here to keep an eye on him. Anybody who gaes him a bad time, has to deal wi' me. Pass the word around."

The man nodded quickly with all the sincerity he could muster in the circumstances. "You never know who you're talking to, do you?"

"Too fucking true, bonzo," said Galloway and left him there.

Back in the bar, he clapped the old man on the back. "Two more doubles, dad, for the troops."

The old man winked in return and seemed to glide across the carpeted floor to the distant horseshoe sweep of mahogany. Galloway watched his long-lost relative with a smile on his face. He was feeling a lot better now. He even could bear to dwell on the events of the early-morning hours in that lock-up garage. Five of them it had taken to give him this. He itemised the damage, putting a name and a face to each of his hurts, for the time when retribution must come. It was important to remember. Remembering each of those young bastards had helped him through the worst of the pain. At the start it was easy, but then as their blood got up, helped on by drink and the sight of him helpless in the chair and taking it, all the kicks and the punches seemed to merge into one, administered not by individuals any more, but by a single great clout coming at him from out of the shadows. He had been luckier than most, he knew that now; most would not have left the place alive. In one corner hung a car's engine-block suspended from a pulley and chain. He recognised its function from something he had read in the papers. On a piece of waste ground, not so long ago, had been found a body with head crushed out of all recognition. He thought too of some of the other methods employed by these same young bloods drunkenly circling him, and tried not to show his true feelings. Ritual murder was a phrase too grand and intellectual for what they spurred each other on to at weekends.

Duff and Tweed watched like two school prefects as the juniors went to work on him. He refused to look at either, even when Tweed, poor soft Tweed, said, "You shouldn't have let him get away from you like that, Ned. Billy says you've put us all at risk," and then another kick slammed into him.

Kells was there, and Tucker, and both delivered their quota, but he had the feeling they might have been holding back. The girl Sharon, however, had a score to settle. "*That fucker hit me once!*" she shrieked, clawing at his cheeks, before the others threw her aside, for she interfered with their own careful workmanship. Towards the end, however, just as in the movies, the squaw was to have her way with him. While the others passed a bottle, she went for his face again. He managed to turn his head, but those nicotine-stained baby fingers ripped the single earring he wore free from the flesh. "What did I tell you?" she cried, holding up the bloody trophy. "A fucking Nazi!"

Remembering, in the bar, Galloway rubbed his lobe. The tiny swastika had been no bigger than the head of a pin. No one had ever remarked on its design before. He had chosen it for that very reason, drawn to the idea of something as discreet as that, his own personal talisman, he believed. The girl, Sharon, had earned the worst punishment of all, because of what she had done. The others would suffer too, of course, in their own way, in good time, but special treatment must be reserved for her. He decided he hated women, all women, and their ways. Now he glanced about the bar, searching for a focus for his hatred. Only one female in the whole place, but she was a pathetic case, her own worst enemy, with that cheap orange-coloured wig and her lipstick drawn across thin lips in a shaky line. The old man was talking to her and he saw them glancing across in his direction.

Presently his ancient friend came back with the drinks and, sure enough, his first words were, "There's a young lady over there who would like to make your acquaintance."

Galloway said, "I don't go with huers," swallowing his whisky in one.

"Oh, Sadie's no pro, young man. She's really a nice girl."

"I can see that from here," then relenting, he squeezed the other's arm, that is, if there was anything resembling flesh and bone hidden in the folds of all that faded army surplus. "I've got to see a man about an Alsatian. Here, you and your girl-friend have a nice time – on me," and pulling out his remaining cash, Galloway dumped it on to the table.

The old man looked down at the heap of notes and silver on the wet wood. He wanted to touch but didn't dare, at least not yet. "You wouldn't be working under cover, would you?" he whispered, glancing about him. "If you are, I want no part of it. I'm strictly neutral, do you hear? I done my bit in North Africa. Once is enough, more than enough, and I want to keep my kneecaps."

Galloway laughed out loud at the worried expression on the lined old face. "Don't alarm yourself. It's only a birthday present."

"But it's not –"

"Let's say you remind me of my old feyther then," and, as though on cue, the dentures were bared in a lingering and foxy grin.

"God bless you, son, you're a white man. Youse all are, all you lads fighting over here on foreign soil."

Outside in the street, Galloway's old dark mood returned, just like the twilight plague of starlings peculiar to this city. Their screams tore at him, as they whirled about the rooftops like blackened scraps of paper. He hunched his shoulders, walking rapidly away from the frenzied cries of creatures uncertain of a billet for the night. He might have to do without himself, he thought.

As far as Bonner and his braves were concerned, he was a dead letter. He looked up at the clock on the leaning Memorial near the docks. In one hour's time, they expected him to be on the boat quietly nosing a passage out into the foggy North Channel. Why should they think differently? He grinned wolfishly, digging fists deeper into the pockets of his old aviator's jacket. It would always be within his power to outwit that crew of vicious boy scouts. Already he had forgotten the humiliation of the early hours and the marks of his ordeal. It was only when a police Landrover swung around a corner and passed him on the deserted street that he realised how conspicuous he might be. He didn't wait for them to retrace their route, taking a second and closer look at the solitary walker. There was a narrow street nearby, closed to traffic, and he turned into it, feeling the imprint of its cobbles through the thin soles of his plimsolls. Woolworth's best, he thought mockingly, for he had never set much store on how he appeared to the world. His leather jacket was the only possession he cared for. It covered him winter and summer, made him feel at one with the cockpit heroes of his youth. But that was private domain, just like the earring. His temples throbbed anew. That girl and her throat, livid with love bites. He would add his own imprint, of that he was resolved.

Ahead of him hung a round red Watney sign; there would be a phone inside. In his head he started rehearsing what he would say when the English voice answered. "If you want the inside story, names, dates, places, all the dope on Billy Bonner and the Brotherhood, I can supply it."

There would be no need for anything further, he told himself. If the hack was worth his salt – and according to what he'd read, he was – *he* would do all the talking from then on. Already Galloway saw himself with a large whisky in his fist, closeted with the famous man in the best suite in the Europa Hotel. On the table between them a small Japanese tape recorder. Notebooks and pencils were relics of the past. He heard his own voice, quietly saying, "I was the number one hit man for –" then he entered the pub.

The place was dim, uncared for, and empty, save for a crone reading the evening paper, which she had spread before her on the counter. He called out, "Phone!" and she pointed to an alcove without looking up from the death notices.

The receiver was already in his grasp, his free hand had dropped to his pocket, when he realised with shock that he had no money. He had given it all away in a fit of arrogance. He looked at the humming handset. To be stymied by the price of a lousy phone call. He dialled one hundred – once, twice, a third time. The delay made him edgy, his voice shook a little when finally he asked for the number of the hotel. He had to repeat his request and, under the pink, unshaded bulb, for the first time felt he was losing control. The writing on the walls of the booth seemed a foreign language. Deeko, Bap, Hendy, Polo, he read. And the cosiness of the operator as though she were speaking from her own kitchen. He hoped it wouldn't be the same one he got when he dialled the second time, but it was.

"Oh, it's you again," she said, and he forced himself to sound humble, "I'm terribly sorry, but I've lost my money in this coin box. It seems to be stuck or something."

"Don't you worry. What number were you dialling? Oh, I know, it was 45161, wasn't it?"

Galloway felt constricted. One of the things he hated most about this country was the so-called friendliness, which everyone took such a great pride in. The pain in their faces whenever you backed away from that bloody great blanket they all wanted to roll you up in. It made his flesh creep thinking of it, and, finally, when his call did get through to the hotel's reception, he was his hard old self again. "Put me through to Mr Clive Morrison. He's expecting the call."

"Could I have your name, please?"

"Never you mind that. Tell him, if he wants the best story he's ever likely to get over here, he'd better get off his bar-stool, pronto. I haven't got all night."

A click followed, then silence on the humming line. At long last a man's voice answered, English, and sounding drunk, as was to be expected. "Yes?"

"Is that Clive Morrison?"

"T'isn't actually. Clive's tied up at the moment. Can *I* help in

117

any way? Something about a story, wasn't there? My name's Bill Bigsby –" and he mentioned another paper.

"Is he in the hotel?"

"No, as a matter of fact. He's at the Ulster Hall. That faith-healer from Detroit, you know. Look here, if the story's a strong one, *our* money's just as good as –"

Galloway stood staring down at the silenced instrument. Then he took out the knife, still warm from his hand, where it had been caressed all along in the lining of his pocket. He pressed the haft and the blade sprang out in readiness, little silver darling. It sliced through the phone wire as though it were soft spaghetti and, leaving the box, he didn't even bother to disguise what shone in his fist.

The woman was still deep in her evening paper, oblivious. His rage was now choking him. He wanted to wield his blade again and again, carving a message for all the world to see and take note of. He was sick of being ignored, when he knew so well his own importance and worth. The woman looked up and saw his white face only when he stabbed down and through her paper and into an inch of the wood beneath. She stared at the quivering steel, then opened her mouth to scream. But the sound refused to come, for the young stranger in the leather jacket, with the marked face, had leaned forward and placed a finger on her lips. She smelt, then tasted, nicotine.

"I seem to have left myself a wee bit short," he said. "What you have in the till should just about cover it." He touched the handle of the knife almost dreamily, watching it vibrate, while the woman fumbled among her takings. "No silver," he called out. "If you don't mind."

She spread the notes before him and he saw a couple of fivers, a handful of soiled ones. Hardly worth the effort, he thought, but then it was the gesture that was important, the cheek of the enterprise. "And one of those wee bottles up on the shelf," pointing to the whisky.

"Scotch?" the woman asked. It was her first word and the gentility of it made him grin, but her eyes were glazed with shock, he could see that. She was working from memory now, until the moment came when she could scream long and loud, letting the relief of it flood over her. Nothing could stop that once it started, he knew that.

At the door he turned and said, "Tell the police to get on to

Billy Bonner about this. *He's* responsible," and closed the door carefully behind him.

The woman stood waiting for the right moment, when she could break down. It was unnatural the way she felt, nothing, no feeling, except the pain in her legs, but that was always with her. The newspaper was still lying open on the counter where she had been reading it when all this started. She looked down at the photograph that spread itself across two of its columns. That other madman that everyone was looking for. In the middle of his forehead was a deep and recent cut. She stared at it, trying to understand how it could have got there. Then the moment finally arrived when she could scream, and she did so, without let-up, until the first police car arrived outside.

15

"YOU SLEEP NOW, do you hear?"

But he hadn't, couldn't, not with that steady, grating roar that came and went like breathing, beyond the thin walls of the bungalow. In the darkness, he could stretch out a hand and prod hollows in its soft sheeting. There was nothing else to do but lie there and imagine water rushing up sloping beds of black pebbles, yet, try as he would, he never could match the rhythm of his own thinking to that other slower, sucking pulse. Was the tide coming in or out, he wondered. Nothing in the sound seemed to provide an answer. He had forgotten just how long the whole business takes, the hours of waiting, before that first hesitant reversal.

Once, four of them had missed every opportunity to fish in a full sea because of the tide-tables and their own ignorance. A week in an ex-army bivvy that let in rain every time a head touched its fine Egyptian cotton. Harvey Spence had supplied the tent, and so they made him lie under the worst leaks because of it. They laughed at his moaning but all knew how he secretly enjoyed being the clown of the party. It was this same stretch of coast too; perhaps a mile or two further north.

He lay inside Nan's sleeping-bag on her folding bed, remembering that week from a past July. His own seventeenth birthday had just passed, unmarked as usual in that house in Berlin Street, and then the holiday week came round for everybody in the Province. He took it for granted then that the whole world shut shop for King Billy's Twelfth, even Catholics, who, if they couldn't get to their work, travelled South to blow their holiday pay in Dublin. That was typical. The empty stout bottles were passed under the flaps, as argument raged in that small tent, but all were in accord when it came to the inherent deceit of the average papish. They could never understand how anyone could be taken in by it – by them. Twenty years later, that same hurt amazement was to affect three-quarters of a population, not just four pimply slum-dwellers aflame with their bigotries in a leaking tent.

Lying there on that camp-bed, he mourned for his lost youth, and for all the others like him. It seemed symbolic to have come full circle to this seaside place. There had never been any escape, really, for the likes of him. The same tides washed over the same dark stones, the same pattern of showers made a week's vacation stretch with boredom. Someone passing on the road, someone young, someone female, could set off fantasies that were always doomed.

And at that moment, incredibly, there were voices outside, girls' voices too. In a panic, he struggled with the fastenings on his bag and, writhing inside its quilted down, fell to the floor. He could smell dust and that other thing too that came from neglect and shuttered rooms. Footsteps sounded on the empty road. One of the girls giggled, another said, "Sssh," then joined in. He strained his ears to hear if there were more. Two only, he decided, and they weren't projections of his imagination, come to haunt him for, "He *did*, I tell you. Honestly." And the words came from someone of flesh and blood, someone who had stopped almost directly outside. "Give us a fag."

"That's two you owe me."

"Big deal," and the plain one giggled. He didn't need his eyes to tell him that. Certain things never changed.

"God, I wish this was pot."

"I bet you wouldn't smoke it."

"You're such a square, Sharon Brown, you really are." Yes, he was right.

In his duck-down cocoon he visualised the two of them sitting on the low wall only yards away, shivering in their dance clothes (he had heard the word disco). Wide baggy trousers, skimpy jackets giving them the look of performing monkeys, the cropped hair, the orthopaedic footwear. But perhaps not so extreme as that. After all, these were country girls, if such existed any more. He felt surprised at how passionate his interest in them had become suddenly. It would be no trouble for him to invent life-histories for these two teenagers, whispering now, for they had entered more private, female territory. "And then he did this . . . and then that . . . and then, and then . . ."

He pressed closer to the fibre wall, trying to catch the intimacies obscured by giggles, feeling himself inflamed, just as he knew they were. Then the final, shocking confidence was delivered. It was inaudible, but the laugh that followed told him as much, and they moved off up the road away from their perch on the wall. He thought of the stones warmed briefly by those young buttocks and, in the depths of the sleeping-bag, felt himself stir.

Old enough to be their father. He could hear them say it with the ease that practice brings – one of a score of hand-me-down catch phrases. Lust was something you learned early on to keep to yourself, for fear of such ridicule.

Harvey had somehow miraculously managed to make a date with a girl that holiday week, he recalled, perhaps because of his clowning. He could always keep a conversation going at a dance, while the rest of them had to struggle around the floor in silence. His winning of the spot-prize clinched his good luck. The locals watched him with suspicion, but even they were disarmed when Harvey waved his box of chocolates at them on a lap of honour. Next evening he only grinned and whistled the more when his partner was called a country heifer and suchlike names. Stooped in the tent, he polished his shoes, then closed the flap on them for the finishing touches to his toilet. When he set out along the road to his waiting date he exuded all the confidence in the world. He didn't seem the old Harvey they knew and had forced to lie under the torn part of the tent.

"He won't get anything."

"He'll say he did."

"Maybe she won't turn up."

"We'll never know."

They looked at one another, then got up and prepared to follow at a careful distance . . .

Stealthily they tracked the great lover to the local landmark called the Butterlump Stone. They scaled its striated flanks until the three of them were immediately above the tongue-tied couple on the grass below. They listened for fireworks to begin, but nothing, not even the soft sounds of grappling; they expected *that*, at least. Craning forward, someone slipped, a piece of stone was dislodged, they were discovered in the act – they, not the two lovebirds – and ran off whooping over the cliff-top pasture back to the camp.

It was a terrible thing, he saw that now, but at the time they hugged themselves with glee. Harvey was not going to be allowed to forget his humiliation. During the daytime he would go off by himself to escape the taunts and when they were drinking together at night no act of vandalism now seemed too extreme for him afterwards on the return journey from the pub. The progression began with the smashing of the porcelain cups on telegraph poles, ending one night when a hay-barn was fired. He kept shouting for more matches, as they ran off, leaving him. Certain things stay in the memory, that was one of them, Harvey outlined against the blaze of that farmer's crop.

Another night, sixteen years later and another image – flames again, but this time in the heart of the city. Harvey again, prancing in front of his handiwork, reeking of petrol.

"Let me, let me," he had pleaded. "Let me burn out the Fenian bastard," when the plan had first been laid in a back room. There should have been some warning in that voice, an echo from the past, but they were all drunk, and he amused them still. Only when they saw his face lit by the blaze did it strike home that here was someone who could put them all behind bars. They tried to pull him away, but he avoided them. He was basking in the great heat like a sun-worshipper. The cracking of glass from inside the chemist's shop and its loudness was another thing that shocked. Presently sirens were heard. They were on the point of leaving him, as they had done that other night, so long ago, in the Antrim countryside, when a screaming horror suddenly presented itself

123

at a top window. It was the chemist himself, the scum they had decided to teach a lesson to, but hadn't reckoned on being on the premises at this late hour. He was ablaze, even his hair, and the sound he made was not to be forgotten. It rang still. This human torch seemed to be looking straight down at them. Then Harvey's courage, or madness, broke, and he rushed off down the street. The rest hung there as though seeing a performance on a bright screen which they must watch to its conclusion.

What happened next was the thing that had eaten away at him like a secret cancer ever since that night ten years ago. The sequence of his actions was precise and sharp in his memory – he was sober, as they all were now – but even if he wasn't, he'd had so much time later to go over and over again that brief span of time, that not a fragment could have been overlooked. He even remembered the damp soaking through the left knee of his trousers as he knelt to take aim. Wherever he went, from that point on, it was as though he carried about with him a burden of images – and ever-growing, as new details were added, smells, sounds, sensations as well. A splinter of glass had gashed his thumb; the tiny pale scar was there still as reminder even if he had no need of one. But what could not be recalled, and that was his penance, was what had passed through his mind as he pulled the trigger. Had he reacted to the man's agony instinctively, or was it merely the culmination of what they had set out to accomplish? In cold blood? Those three words had locked him away for "the term of his natural life". Everyone seemed to be using it suddenly, after they had all been lifted a week later: that's how long it had taken Harvey's nerve to go. Police, the prosecution, the newspapers and finally the weak politician who had decided to make a stand to save his reputation. There was the spectacle of him on television trying to shape his features into an expression of righteous anger over the case, when all that came across was the face of someone showing well-bred distaste for everyone and everything connected with his job. He and his kind were the real enemy, not that poor gun-running chemist bastard, yet they were still being shot, stabbed, beaten to death out there by replicas of his former self. And *he* was loved for being the original. The sight of his own name on walls, that was what had opened up all the old wounds.

It had been said at the time, and since, that he was the ringleader, evil genius at the back of the business, his decision

124

and his alone to set fire to the shop *after* the victim had been riddled. And as though the idea was too perfect in its purity to be sullied by the slightest scrutiny, everyone – even those charged with him – accepted it as fact. They were so convincing that even he had to wonder if he hadn't been suffering delusion. Could he have transposed the events to make them more bearable?

Later he had managed to question Patton and Maxwell in prison (Maxwell had done some sort of deal and was now in Canada) but they were still confused about what had happened, not positive as they had been made out to be. They looked at him with hurt in their eyes and they were much worse off than he was, he could see that. He had set himself the task then of finding the truth the hard way, the only way, by himself, in the confines of his own head, sifting, weighing, rejecting and, finally, hoarding the tiniest of clues. This archaeology of the mind had become a constant pursuit. No, he had fired *after* the blaze, he no longer questioned that as fact, but the final sherd was still missing. *Why* had he pulled the trigger when he did? Only he, it seemed, cared any more.

Every man carries about with him a question to be answered about himself. It can be a doubt about his legitimacy, or his wife's faithfulness, or even the size of his equipment. He had his too. It usually asserted itself after enough drink. No drop had touched his own lips for a good ten years however. There was a bottle of spirits on a small table in the corner, along with the food Nan had left him. She had joked about the tin-opener, saying that and the hard stuff were all he would need on his desert island.

When she was living at home, her parents came here every summer, she said. The long holidays were the best time of her life, until she got too old for sand-castles. He had a sudden pang, thinking she might have passed by a small khaki tent in its hollow beside the road, one wet week in July. That she came from people who owned a holiday home impressed him, but she laughed in that loud, open way of hers. The place had been little more than a shack when they had first bought it. Her handyman father had spent all his spare time adding bits here, bits there. His babby house, she called it.

"And now look at it." They were together in the double sleeping-bag, clinging moistly. Her odour, her bulk, the taste of sweat, scent and vodka all conspired to swamp him, but he could see what she meant. The metal legs of the folding bed, inches from his face – the bag was on the floor – had ploughed tracks in the accumulated dust of what must have been years.

"Twenty, at least," she murmured. Leaning on one bare beautiful elbow now, she puffed out smoke from the ritual cigarette. He lay where he was. Could such luck hold?

"Oh, fuck it and him along with it! He was a tight old bastard, always skimping so he could put up another wee shelf."

He felt overcome by the soft, sweet geometry surrounding him. She looked down smiling. "You have revived, haven't you?" feeling his exploratory touch resume beneath the covers.

He had taken the initiative this second time, surprising them both, when they first arrived. Allowing herself to be fumbled, then manoeuvred inexpertly down on to the spread, unzipped bag, she laughed at his seriousness, but, moments later, when her breath quickened, he enjoyed his reward. In a sort of sly amazement at his own handiwork, he steered this perfect craft towards landfall. His mouth covered hers, for he was afraid her cry might carry beyond the thin walls. His own climax, muted but pleasurable, followed.

They lay bonded together. It was late afternoon. The dying sun fell through a space between the curtains – they were little more than rags – and motes, stirred up by their recent activity, danced in its beam. Beyond the sea-wall outside, the waves rose and fell in sympathy with their own slowing pulses. Everything seemed simple.

"Nice," she murmured, tightening her hold. There was no need for him to answer. "*Our* babby house, eh?"

He felt as though something inside himself had suddenly started to shift and, finally, after all this long time, he allowed emotion its rein. He wept like a child, and the image was apt, because he heard his own voice jerking out fragments of complaint at the unfairness of everything. She had comforted him and then, finally, leaving him, promising to return next day, she had said, "You sleep now, do you hear?"

16

THE HALL that Ned Galloway was seeking – the one that the journalist had mentioned on the phone – was in one of the wide streets radiating from what they liked to call, here, the City Centre, for no real reason that Galloway could ever appreciate. Once upon a time, he understood, trams turned at the spot, then went back the way they had come, to places with names like Bellevue, Bloomfield, Cliftonville, Fortwilliam, Belmont. If he had thought about it – and he didn't much, seeing himself as a transient – the names would only have reinforced his contempt for all those soft suburbanites apeing the English. In his own savage way he rejoiced to see their pretensions brought down, just as their capital had been. The bombers seemed to be bent on reducing the place to one vast car-park, it struck him, as he moved swiftly across an empty, brick-strewn expanse between two new buildings, one an insurance block, the other a glittering bank. This was the way they fought each other here on this ugly battlefield, the power of a car-boot packed with explosives pitted against big business. What if the two were secretly in league – for they seemed to feed off one another? It wouldn't surprise him, nothing would here, for there was that distinct feeling always in the air that somewhere palms were being greased. He remembered the bar he had been in earlier, men with their heads close, the way they had of looking up suddenly each time the door would open. And everyone carrying his own thick wad of spending-money. That too had not escaped him.

Galloway sheltered for a moment in the lee of the solitary yellow wooden hut guarding the parking lot and thought bitterly that he should have got his own hands on some of those floating assets, before cutting himself adrift. Or being cut adrift, he corrected, to wander across the face of this dead, planetary place. But somehow the idea of himself as that lonely voyager in battered old leather jacket transformed his mood. The anger was still there certainly, even though still diffuse; as yet, he had no single object to focus its force, but by now the fires had been banked down to a controlled heat. The night was cold for September, but as he hurried, bent on his way, he could almost fancy there to be a glow within.

Presently he came to the first of the posters that were to lead him to his destination, like the white stones in that fairytale he had once read, only this was here and now in a strafed wilderness of rubble, broken glass and squashed beer cans, all bearing the same vicious imprint, it seemed.

Have These Hands The Power To Heal? he read, and underneath, a photograph of the famous man's manicured mitts, reputed, so the papers said, to be insured for more than Liberace's or Christian Barnard's. They were everywhere now, those outstretched, slightly limp paws, signalling from every stretch of wall, even wrapped around poles and lamp-posts. Their owner had arrived in the city that morning in his own private plane. He had been on television, leaking sticky good will, in a white suit, white shirt, white tie. Only his face had a Florida tan. The camera stayed on his lap for most of the interview, as though expecting a miracle.

Galloway crossed two streets, another cleared space, then came round a corner and stopped short. At first he thought the crowd outside the hall were the faithful fighting to get in, but then he saw the fire-engine and the lazy circling blue lights and realised this was an exodus. Men and women – the latter in greater evidence – flailed their way out through the open doors in a dense mob, then overflowed across the street to mingle around the waiting ambulances and tenders. All panic seemed to leave them once they had struggled free of that packed funnel on the steps. In vain the police tried to move them back, clearing a broad space. Tape fluttered in a constable's hand in readiness, but these people, dressed for church, seemed reluctant about being too easily diverted from their expectation. Galloway noticed some limped on short metal crutches; others, grown men and women, were led by the hand like children.

Then the mob seemed to quicken, and for the first time the noise they made registered with the man watching from the shadows. It rose in the air to drown the shrill cries of the starlings, disturbed from their roosting places on the ledges and gutters of the buildings all about. A part of the crowd began to run back to the hall to a side door which had now opened. They had sighted a white suit and nothing the police could do could hold them back. Galloway felt he was witnessing something he might easily read about in the morning papers. A man with a camera started flashing his bulbs and, as though on cue, others in the crowd, who had so far held back, now began running and hobbling forward. At the photographer's elbow was someone in a pale waterproof, who was pointing quickly at sections of the crowd. Galloway felt certain this was the man he was seeking. He hadn't the look of a believer or someone who would need the laying-on of hands with his shortie raincoat and his Russian fur hat and that complexion. Even at this distance he could see it had the look and colour of prime beef.

He decided he must get close, but that was no longer easy. A wide no-man's-land had now opened up between his quarry and the crowd struggling to get near the man in tropical garb. The police were there as well and more would be arriving at any moment, to judge by the crackling of walkie-talkies, which they held clasped to their cheeks.

But then suddenly Galloway's problem was resolved in a way which he had not foreseen. For a brief moment the cries of the birds were magically silenced; it was as though a space had been scooped out of the atmosphere, but then, as though to fill that vacuum, the bomb went off and its detonation flung him to his knees. The air was full of flying slates and brick-dust, papers were sucked up out of litter-bins, something struck him on the cheek, he felt blood, looked down and saw what looked like a small cog-wheel, the kind usually associated with the inner mechanism of a clock. Without thinking, he picked it up and put it in his pocket. Later, that tiny, toothed thing was to become a source of almost childish wonder to him. He would finger it, obsessively imagining its history. It put him in mind of those school compositions they always set, with titles like, "The Story Of A New Penny" or "A Gentleman's Watch".

But that was in the future, now it was something else that absorbed him. For a moment he believed he had been deafened. His eyes told him there should have been screams and shouting, for the space in front of the hall was now thickly covered with men and women lying or crawling among debris. One or two had even managed to stand or remain standing, like stumps in a felled wood, but no sound came from them either. A great silence cupped the entire quarter. Then there reached Galloway's ears a strange and eerie noise, the like of which he had never experienced before. It was as though a million brittle icicles were breaking off in tiny particles, the tinkling magnified in the still air. The glass was falling out of every pane in every building right around the square, and as the fragments started to rain almost gently down the screaming began.

Galloway shook his head to clear his brain. Now the scene rushed at him, he saw blood on faces, limbs at odd angles, several of the police, hatless, on hands and knees. The faith-healer's aides were smashing in the windscreen of his car, so that they could see to drive away. *Their* senses had returned fastest of all.

But someone else was aware also – perhaps this different sound of breaking glass had alerted him to his duties. The man in the raincoat, still wearing his Moscow hat, was moving as quickly as he could manage it through the stricken towards the big dented limousine. He reached it and Galloway saw him waving something, a piece of paper it looked like. There was no sign of the great man. They must have got him into the back of the car by now.

Galloway realised this was the moment he had been waiting for. He moved out from the lee of the wall and immediately was a part of the turmoil. He tried not to look closely at the faces or heed the cries; at all costs he must keep his sights on his goal. What shook him most however was the uncovered thighs of the women, all modesty abandoned in a sprawl of pink and white underwear that his own mother might have worn. That these same women were moaning or frozen in shock didn't somehow affect him. Stepping over them whenever he had to, he drew closer to the group gathered about the car. They didn't even notice him standing there, those three well-built charmers in suits just a shade darker than their master's, who was urging them to hurry, from the confines of the car.

"*Break it open, for Christ's sake!*" Galloway heard him call out as they tugged at the jammed door. "And let's get out of this bleedin' place." What surprised most was not the profanity, but that the American accent had gone completely.

The man in the fur hat didn't seem to have noticed the ringing tones of Bow Bells, he was struggling to force his head into the car.

"You must get out! Think of the story! My god, *just think of it!*"

Galloway touched his arm – already two of the police were picking their way towards them. "Mr Morrison?" But the scent of a scoop, so unthinkable, so amazing, had never been so strong in the other's nostrils. "Mr Morrison. *Please.*" He hated himself for saying it, but he had to. Again he put his hand out, the bobbies were in the middle of the square by now; he squeezed. He felt the arm stiffen, as did the rest of the hack under his soiled rainproof. A face almost purple in its fury swung round. "Piss off – whoever you are!" then head and shoulders were thrust back through the jagged window opening once more.

In his pocket, Galloway's grip tightened instinctively on the smooth handle of the knife. The bulk mere inches away drew him as though from genuine affection. A hand laid in friendly fashion on that shoulder, the move closer, blade sliding in, so easily, so swift, and at the end the reward of seeing the other's face, a look that said, "I didn't know. Why? Why?" The only sort of real apology that would suffice.

But one of the running, stumbling policeman shouted, "*Hey!*" and the intention withered. He moved quickly away, found the mouth of a darkened street leading from the scene, and soon glass no longer crackled beneath his feet. It was as though all the damage to life and limb and property he had witnessed hadn't really happened. All of it had been wiped from his mind just by a change of scene. But perhaps it wasn't really that, no, perhaps it was because something else had usurped its place, something much more potent.

131

As he hurried along, he hugged the thought of vengeance to himself, and words came, *people will pay, people will pay*, almost a refrain. Another had been added to the growing list, a pig in a fur hat, a pig who had turned down the story of a lifetime because he was too piggish to lift his snout from the trough to see what was being offered to him. That time when he was about to stick him, it would have been like butchering bacon.

He stopped to take a swig from the stolen whisky. Afterwards his mouth felt sour. His mood too underwent a change. Who was he kidding, he told himself, there was no way he was going to be able to get back at all these people. He only enjoyed the idea of it, that's what it boiled down to, like some poor fantasising prick who had seen too many bad movies and carried the plots about in his head with him wherever he went. Bonner, Duff, Tweed, the girl Sharon, friend Morrison, they might as well be something glimpsed on a screen, for all they affected him and his dreams of revenge. Reality wasn't like the *Ten Little Niggers*, and he was no avenging genius in a dinner suit, either. Reality was this alley-way, the taste of bad booze in his throat, and having no immediate plans, no plans of any sort. In a moment of cruel clarity he saw his fate, the path the future was mapping out for him, down which he would stumble to the final resting place. His home city, after all, had given more dedicated drinkers to the world than any other. Why not let history take its course? He was kidding himself again, the drink doing his thinking for him.

Taking the enemy by its narrow cold neck, he flung it hard against a far wall. The sound of more glass breaking would be neither here nor there on such a night. Then he moved on; the idea had come to him that being stationary gave rise to too much thinking, and of the morbid variety too. But in spite of his speed — he was turning into each strange new street as he came to it without purpose — the thoughts would keep on breaking like bubbles in his brain. They followed each other in streams, linked like those silvery chains that rise from the bottom of soda syphons. Thoughts, images, faces, then one face, a gaunt and unsmiling one. It suddenly struck home just how unsmiling. Not once had a flicker of amusement of any sort crossed that suffering mug. He sweated with shame realising that he had tried, he, Galloway, to make jokes, to coax some reaction out of that man in his mockery of a suit, the one he had at first despised, then had grown to be interested in, had finally imagined shared some affinity. And all this time, all those times, he had joked or swaggered, that same old grey man had been sizing *him* up, despising *him*: all along.

There was an ache in his head as the full horror of that truth drove home. It stopped him as though he had run up against something as solid as brick or stone, yet here he was in the middle of an empty street somewhere in a part of the city he didn't know. He felt cautious in an instant. It was a warning. To continue with this same line of conduct would surely lead to the ultimate stupidity. He allowed himself to drift over from the brow of the street where he had been proceeding on an arrogant course, until he was walking on the pavement like any law-abiding citizen.

For the first time he noticed that he had strayed into a residential area of avenues where trees grew at intervals, where the parked cars looked as though they might be hosed down and waxed on Sunday mornings. He took his hands out of his pockets and straightened his shoulders. There was nothing to be done about his looks, at any rate. His pace was now purposeful; loitering, with or without intent, an accusation no one watching could bring against him. Yet, he *had* intent now, he had that, sure enough.

He started to walk much faster again as though to keep pace with all the ideas forcing themselves into his head. He felt he could see events and people as never before and the effect they had on him and the way things had turned out for him. All his hatreds were at last converging on their target.

He had no idea how far he must have walked before he found the street he was searching for. He felt no fatigue. That, too, like the fact that he seemed to head unerringly through areas he had never ventured into before, to a street he had only visited once, was the product of his new state. There was an alleyway lined with black bags of refuse. He picked his way carefully past – they looked as though they might burst at any instant – until he reached a door. It was unpainted and he could see no handle or even a lock. That shook him a little. He looked forward, then back, but there was no sign of any other opening. He closed his eyes as he stood there on rotting skins the better to bring back a picture of that day when he had sat in the car parked across the mouth of the entry, while Billy Bonner had tiptoed away from them. It was that image of Bonner picking his steps that decided him. No, he

133

had made no mistake, this was the place.

He began to feel with his hands along the edges of the door as if the right touch might somehow spring it open. Then his fingers found a bell-push and he almost laughed aloud at any doubts he might have had. His old luck had returned, so why should he worry? Still, before pressing the discreet little button, he stepped back and passed his hands through his short thatch, useless as this gesture was bound to be. He rang the bell. There was a long pause, but he waited patiently, knowing someone would come. He heard a voice; he almost laughed, it was so timid, a girl's voice.

"Who is it?"

"A friend of Billy's," he said and that was risky, he supposed, because he did not know who or what awaited him on the other side of the deal door. A longer pause followed and no movement that he was aware of. He knew whoever had spoken was thinking out the next move. That gave him certainty and he said, "Hurry up, sweetheart! Don't keep the customers waiting!" A bolt was slid across, a crack appeared, he saw eyes, part of a face. That was enough for him; he pushed on the door, driving the girl before him.

The opulence of the room shocked him, certainly he had not expected anything quite like this, and as he stood there blinking a little, his confidence left him. Such surroundings always made him conscious of his appearance, his origins. The girl was eyeing him; she had retreated behind the fancy desk. He saw there was a row of buttons. Keeping his attention on her hands, he said, "You're new here, aren't you, love?" It was a shot in the dark, but not quite. Her nervousness somehow didn't belong to someone who sat here each day filing her nails, servicing the patrons almost automatically. Did she even know who Billy Bonner was, he wondered.

"It's all right, sweetheart, I've got the readies," and he pulled out his clutch of paper money. That was a wrong move and he regretted it instantly, for it denoted eagerness on his part. But the girl didn't seem to notice.

"I'm only here temporary. The girl who's usually here is away. She didn't come in today. I usually work – upstairs." She faltered as though her tongue had betrayed her, but Galloway, with barely a hesitation, said, "That's a pity, for you're just my type," and in a way it was true. She could have been any one of a score or more of similar little scrubbers, who all quivered under him like she-fowl,

134

when it came to the short and not particularly urgent moment.

"Look," he said, "can I sit down?"

"Yes, yes," she said, but he had already lowered himself into the depths of a leather settee. It sighed under him, exuding newness. The whole place had the look of a shop-window display; only the two dummies were all wrong, and both of them knew it.

"What's your name?"

"Mandy," she said. She was a nail-biter, he could see that.

"Mandy," he began slowly, "a pal of mine paid a call not so long ago, a good friend, and he couldn't speak too highly of the treatment he received. Now, knowing him, I'm prepared to bet you were the very wee lassie who . . . who fixed him up. We have similar tastes, you understand? Would I be wrong?"

She was smiling. My god, this was so easy, he thought.

"What did your friend look like? Was he Scotch – like you?"

"No. I'll tell you his name though, if you like."

"Oh, we never use names here."

Her own tiny quota of self-importance was coming back. Idiots like this deserved everything that was coming to them, blonde little dollies with pushed-out pointed tits and baby-blue eyes that rolled about in their head. He became impatient to reach the moment when he could dispense with pleasantries. "You'd remember this chap all right. Big with white hair. Premature. More – *silver*, you might call it."

The eyes blinked desperately, began to slide and shift. Jackpot, he thought. "Come on," he coaxed. "He's a buddy of mine. We share everything – if you see what I mean."

"It's not allowed," she whispered.

He rose from the settee. "Come on. Surely you can oblige? Things are slack at the moment." His hands now were flat on the desk. The smell of powder and cheap perfume didn't quite mask that other scent he recognised. People sweat with fear. Galloway smelt fear, even if his eyes didn't already tell him so. His hand touched her cheek, patted it the way you would a child's. She shrank but didn't move from his touch.

"If it's a matter of money," he murmured, even though he knew it wasn't.

"I can't."

"Can't? You mean, won't."

The next pat on the cheek was a little harder. Then he put his hand on her breast, felt the construction that cheated those little things she had out to two points that were meant to be provocative. There was nothing there really, yet she moaned a little. This one would do it for love, he thought. A real little amateur; he knew the sort. He was filled with disgust at her willingness. Images were swamping him again. Two on a bed; her, with her clothes off, all that inadequacy on show finally, and no shame – and *him*. He remembered the thin stick legs, had seen him bent over a basin later, his back bare, arched, a line of bumps like strung beads.

"It wasn't me," she was saying, "it wasn't me," over and over again.

He shook his head as though to clear away the foulness he had let flourish there.

"It was someone else."

"Someone else?"

"Yes, yes, yes. One of the other girls."

His hand shook, the one touching her. He took it away. He needed a smoke badly, but he couldn't, he would spill it all over the floor, the carpet. He looked down at the pattern, felt the reality of the room and everything in it take hold again. The settee sighed under him. "Oh?" he said. It sounded like a weak echo.

"Yes," she said, anxious to tell. "One of the other girls."

"Is she upstairs now?"

What he had come all this way for was now within his grasp, yet all the driving force seemed to have left him. He couldn't explain it.

"No."

"What do you mean, no. Don't play games. I haven't the time."

"Honestly. She's off sick, or something. I told you. She's the one who stays down here."

"*All* the time?"

"Yes."

He looked at her, yet not really seeing all that thinness padded and puffed out, the hair lacquered until it had the consistency of wire-wool, the eyes outlined in blues and blacks, fingers thickened with cheap rings.

"She never works upstairs. Never. Wouldn't know how to, if you ask me." She permitted herself a little laugh, then cast glances at him. "Here, would you like a drink?"

Galloway moved his head as though it had suddenly become

very heavy. Things had taken on a new and disturbing meaning. "This girl –" he began.

"You wouldn't like her. Honest. Stuck up. Thinks she's a cut above the rest."

The phrase stung. Two of a kind, he thought. "Her name," he said.

"Aw, listen, she's not worth bothering about. None of us even know why she ever went with your friend."

Friend, he thought bitterly. He lost all patience. It was facts, facts he craved. Later he could fit them together, not now, not here in this blinding room where he felt like a piece of rubbish that somehow had been tramped in from the mire of the alleyway outside. He belonged there, didn't he? Yes, he did, and a terrible perverse pride took hold. She saw it in his face, or something akin to it, that frightened her.

"Nan. That's her name. Nan Harding," she blurted.

He sat on the couch, and questioned calmly. An address? No, no, she was genuinely sorry about that, but there might just be a phone number somewhere, somewhere. There was a list, she had seen it once. All their numbers were on it, her own included. Calls had to be made if a special customer wanted to come without an appointment. Friends of Billy Bonner's. She looked at him, but he said nothing. The list was found, in a drawer, and she wrote the number down carefully for him on a piece of paper. He took it from her and then, copying an old movie trick, he pushed a couple of notes down the front of her dress. She clung to him and he put up with it.

"Look," he heard her whisper, "maybe I could go upstairs, if you want."

"No," he said, "I've got to get back to the wife," and, although he smiled at the idea, there was really a sort of twisted truth about that. Even he had to have somewhere to lay his head.

He left her then, standing in the centre of that bright room that made both of them look and feel so out of place. They were of the same tribe and each knew it and in his own cruel intuitive way he could imagine her little spasm of misery after he had gone. He left her something.

"I'll be back," he said, not meaning it. "You and I have some unfinished business – blondie."

"Is that a threat or a promise?" Her voice was soft.

"Both, darling. Both," he said.

All the way back across the city to his own personal bolt-hole, Ned Galloway carried with him the satisfaction of the encounter. It hung about him like a scent, to be savoured over and over again. Even when he finally arrived at the prefab near the Waterworks, his mood was still high. He felt no depression – a natural reaction at the sight of the structure with its streaked grey walls and roof and the windows, deprived of glass, it seemed, since its very first construction. Bombs had fallen from the skies then, now they were planted secretly like seeds that flowered suddenly at their own lethal whim.

A light was still on and he made for it across the patch of broken ground that someone had once dug for victory. He pushed the back door open and all within was as he'd left it, the wallpaper hanging in strips – the brat's handiwork – the cracked lino, the three-piece suite rescued from the roadside dump, all lit by a single fly-specked bulb. It was very different from the room he had just left, but he felt more assured here, and reassurance came also from the familiar face and person of the figure in one of the armchairs. It was as though she hadn't moved since his last visit to make use of her and her miserable dwelling. Not that she would ever think of it in such terms – in any terms – for she rarely spoke. Now she rose and padded into the scullery, where, in her usual subdued way, she moved some pots about on top of the stove.

Galloway flung himself on the sofa and uncorked a bottle. The last inch of whisky seemed to have lost most of its potency, yet it still lulled. Then she brought him beans on toast, still without speaking, and after he had wiped the plate clean, he motioned to her to come across to where he lay. He felt almost affectionate, the way you might towards some dumb thing. Looking down on her bent head, as she nuzzled dutifully, he thought of the other blonde. He gave himself over to a brief fantasy, the two heads alternating, pleasuring him in turn. Then, abruptly, he pushed one of them away from him – the flesh and blood one – buttoning himself.

After she had gone to bed in the other room, where the brat had its cot, Galloway prised up a loose floorboard only he knew about. From its hiding place down among the dry rot he took out the old metal ammunition case. Locked away inside were his few treasures – the S.S. dagger, the medals, a red and black armband, his passport, money, a few snaps from the old Cyprus and Aden days, but now there was an addition. A book. He opened it at random. *"They are pushing us into this struggle; there is no alternative; we must prepare it and we must decide to undertake it."* The passage was underlined. The hand of the man he was hunting in earnest now had made those marks, as carefully as though they had been drawn with a ruler. It was only a tiny speck of insight, yet he would store up any grains such as he could lay his hands on, Galloway told himself. This night he had come across a regular nugget. Unfolding the scrap of blue notepaper, he read the telephone number the girl had written there, until he had memorised it. Then he put the folded slip between the leaves of the book at the place where he had opened it. *"They are pushing us into this struggle . . ."*

He went to sleep with the phrase hammering in his head. In some odd way, it linked him evenly more closely to his quarry, for Ned Galloway could understand all too well the potency of those words. Once more the strange duality of his feelings towards the one who had brought him to his present state perplexed and disturbed him, but finally sleep came on that broken-backed settee. The light still burned weakly. He couldn't be bothered to rise and cross to the switch.

17

"A PERFECT DAY for a picnic," she said. "But if we can't have it out there, we'll just have to have it in here."

He watched her spread the delicacies she had brought with her out on the open sleeping-bag. There were packets and portions of strange things in tubs he had never seen or tasted before, fruit and two bottles of pink wine. They drank from paper cups and he enjoyed her enjoyment. "You shouldn't have spent all your money," he said.

"To hell with it," she said. "I only wanted the excuse."

He felt the wine relaxing and warming. "We eat and drink all the wrong things in this country," he said. It was the sort of statement someone else might have made in some other, perfectly normal situation, yet he didn't care or even think about it.

"I know," she replied, "but the weather's not always the way it is today."

Outside the sun beat down on a flat, silver sea which barely whispered as it fell on shingle. The air was still as only it can be at the approach of autumn, and a jet trail high above slowly unravelled into flakes of the purest white. They drifted off and were gone and, with the second bottle, it seemed as though the phenomenon was somehow natural, yet amazing, at the same time. Both of them were feeling and thinking the same things, he could tell. They lay back among the debris of the meal and the plumped-out nylon of the bag was cool where it touched their skin. They began to talk about the old days, places and faces.

"Do you remember the wee man who used to play the saw outside the Water Office?"

"I do," he said. "And what about Old Corky?"

They laughed, remembering a terror from their youth.

"And there used to be a man always on the march in big army boots."

"His hair cropped?"

"That's right." Yes, there were always lonely men who walked long distances in their city, out from the streets and off up into the quiet hilly parts every day in all weathers. Sometimes they had a dog, usually not. He wondered if that too had all changed.

"We should have met each other then," she said.

"I wasn't your class," he said, and he felt it still, despite all the books he'd read.

She looked at him. "I thought you didn't believe in any of that."

"It's something you don't get rid of all that easily. We were all second-class citizens . . . and didn't know it."

"Is that what all this present bother's about then?" She was mocking him, he knew, but the wine had softened both their reactions.

"My belief is that it is – deep down."

"Deep down," she murmured. Her hand had slipped under his shirt. "Big boy, you need somebody to look after you."

"Feed me up?" His turn now to smile at her.

"Put some hair on your chest."

He kissed her and again felt amazed at how easily all this came to him. The sea murmured, sea birds cried distantly, a car droned past every twenty minutes or so in no particular haste. He felt as though all the urgency he had stored up over the years was slowly leaking away. Why couldn't they stay like this? That thought also amazed him – or was it only the wine?

Then, being a woman, she became brisk, impatient with

dreams, needing actions. "We've got to get you out of here. But, first, you need a doctor." She looked at him. "A serious condition. It said so in the paper."

A serious condition, that just about covers it, all right, he thought to himself. "I feel fine," he told her. That was true enough. The ache in his temples had gone. "And anyway I couldn't just walk into some surgery. Could I now?"

"I suppose not," she said. "But if you have to –"

"You'll be the first to know."

He felt the implications of his words the instant they left his lips. Melodramatic as it might sound, his very life rested in the hands of this woman now facing him. He looked at her in a new way. She was biting into a pear and its juices trickled down her chin. Her teeth were large, white and capable, like the rest of her. He thought of the wound they might inflict. It was a strange thought to have at that moment, but it made him resolve secretly not to give up everything of himself. Some betrayal might yet be necessary.

"Why are you doing all this for me?"

Sighing, she said, "Why can't you just accept it?"

"Because I have no choice, is that it?"

"No, it isn't. Believe me."

Her eyes were soft. There were the beginnings of pouches, he noticed, fine lines also, the result of too many cigarettes. The forties would be her bad time. They approached fast. She probably knew it. "Tell me. Now," he said.

"I can't. I don't know why. It seemed a good idea at the time . . . and," hastily, "still does. Mad, but good. And now that I'm in . . . well . . ."

They looked at one another. "Women," he sighed.

She laughed. "It's not a man's world any more, you know." She paused. "Where you came from it still is though, isn't it? Boys' town?"

"Is that how you see it? Us?" Her fingernail, red as blood, gently scratched his chest, a feminine distraction. He held the moving hand still. "I want to know."

She drained her paper cup, then flung it into a dark corner. It could lie there, a soiled memento of their visit, for an eternity, he thought. Then she answered him.

"If you must know, we're sick and tired of the lot of you, and all you stand for!"

Above their heads a spider hung suspended in its dusty gossamer. A car passed and the spider bounced gently, as on an invisible trampoline. When all movement had ceased, he spoke quietly, "You blame us for everything that's happened. That's too easy."

"Who should we blame then? For all the violence?"

"That was there all along. We're a violent people. Look at us. Listen to us . . . This country came out of violence. It sits on the brink. Yet everyone's always amazed when it breaks out again – every time."

She looked at him. "Some people think you were the one who pulled the trigger first – *this* time."

"Do *you* believe that?"

She moved her body awkwardly on the blue quilting as though it had suddenly become very heavy. "I don't know what to believe." Then, quickly touching him, she said, "I believe what you tell me."

He remembered the manner of their first meeting in that upstairs room, with the pink net on its windows, her oiled hands working on him clumsily, her panicked pleas finally, the tears. Something of that same susceptibility had leaked into the room they were now lying in and, as before, he felt the urge to inflict hurt.

"*We're* not the ones who should be in cages. It's you lot, from what I've seen. The real animals – the Billy Bonners and Co – the man you work for. You *do* take his money, don't you? Don't you?"

Her large eyes rested on him. "Not any more," she said. "But I thought you two were buddies."

"Billy Bonner is scum. He's living on borrowed time."

"But he was the one who –"

"That's right," he said quickly, "that's right. But it was *his* idea . . ." He was angry suddenly. For what reason, he asked himself, because of Billy Bonner, or was it really because he had betrayed something painful of himself?

"Well, in that case," she snapped, "maybe you should go back. If you hate it so much on this side of the fence. Hate *us* so much."

He wanted to smile in spite of himself, but daren't, remembering those strong teeth and the intimation he had had earlier. "I don't hate *you*, Nan," he said. "I couldn't ever do that." His hand took hold of hers. She looked down at the image they made together on the blue nylon. He hoped she wouldn't recognise too

143

much incompatability there – at least, not just yet.

"Don't go back," she said softly.

"Is there a choice?"

She knelt before him, excited now like a schoolgirl. "Listen," she said. "I've thought of a way, a way . . . out. Somewhere you, we both, can go. You'd like that, wouldn't you?"

Yes, he thought, he would like that. He felt tired now, and the thought was an equally tired one. Was that a pain beginning in his head again?

"I know they'll be looking for you at the airport, and at all the cross-channel ferries too, but we can still get across the Border. Can't we?"

He looked at her. "True," he said. "But what happens at the other end? When I step off the boat at Holyhead or Fishguard with my little brown paper parcel – or even the plane at Heathrow?"

"You don't. You stay where you are. In the South."

The South. As foreign to him and his tribe as another continent. Badlands.

"Nobody can touch you down there. Isn't it true? Isn't it?"

"Touch me?" He smiled, yet he knew what she was getting at. Political prisoners – and he must be considered one, surely – couldn't be extradited for crimes committed in his, the northern part of the island. His native cynicism told him that that convenience had not been written into the Constitution for runaways of his colour. He might make an interesting test case – that was, if he survived long enough among all the other refugees with accents like his own, but different politics and creeds, already there. And they, of course, had a ready source of income.

"What do we do for money?" he said. "Rob banks? Bonnie and Clyde? *Us?*" He hoped she'd laugh at the idea of that.

She didn't. "God, and I thought you were the brains of your outfit! The great dynamic force."

"You know what they say. In the land of the blind the one-eyed man is king."

Did he really mean that, he thought? It was curious, how being with her seemed to send him off into questioning and questionable areas he hadn't ventured near for years – if ever. Certainly not while he had been measuring out that other existence against its background of regulations and routine, developed purposely to deaden the more private thought processes. He felt like a tap that had been turned on after a long interval of disuse. He looked about him. Perhaps he was really only making excuses so as not to have to leave his dusty cave, where all he wanted, now, it seemed, was to be alone and think things out for himself, let that tap flow long and freely ...

She said, "What do you want to do? Sit here and rot? Is that it? Or take a chance?"

She had forgotten there was a third alternative, and he decided not to remind her. "I'll take my chances – with you, Nan."

She softened at the mention of her name, and, noting it, so dispassionately, as he did, it seemed to him that he had already started off down that easy road to betrayal.

For the rest of the dying afternoon she talked excitedly, and he listened. They could take her car, she said, going across the border at night on one of the unapproved roads. And, as an added precaution – and here she giggled – she had hit on the scheme of plastering their Beetle with *Just Married* signs. Confetti would come in handy also. She laughed even louder, then, to his amazement, she took out of her bag a canister of the stuff and, there and then, sprinkled it over his head and shoulders. He sat there on the sleeping-bag looking at her.

She choked, "Just look at the groom, would you, in his going-away clothes," and, after a moment, he laughed a little as well. She brushed most of it from his hair and he caught her and then they embraced, lying together among the sliding drifts of tiny paper discs on their turquoise ground. It surprised him to think of her planning so ingeniously on his behalf, while he brooded in his dusty cave; that did surprise him. But, as they made love, the thought came to him also that other people out there beyond the thin walls must be laying their plans for him as well.

18

"AND WHAT'S YOUR NUMBER, CALLER?"

"731400."

"And your name, caller?"

"Harding. You must be sending the bills out to the wrong address."

"Just a moment, caller." A pause and then the adenoidal voice was back on the line again. "Well, caller, the address we've got down here for you is . . ."

It was as easy as that, and Ned Galloway permitted himself a wink and a grin at the reflection in the phone-box mirror. It grinned and winked back. Jekyll and Hyde, he thought; but, today, he was the well behaved one. Witness his polite tones of a moment ago. "I wonder if you can *possibly* help me . . ." He even held the door of the kiosk open for a woman who looked at him suspiciously, and then after him, through the smeared glass, as he strolled away whistling.

Down through the Gardens he went, past the stepped cascade of yellowish water. Three pensioners stared at the gliding currents as though determined not to miss something momentous that would enrich their day. They didn't even break their gaze as he marched past, but on this bright, new morning his was a passable appearance. Soap, water and a comb had transformed the bloodstained hooligan of the night before into just another corner-boy.

When he reached the railings where the roar of early-morning traffic came in steady waves, he slowed his pace. All these cars, buses, lorries, carried people. It would be foolish to stroll along under their gaze. What was worse, however, was that directly across from the park were the mouths of a mesh of streets, which stretched down to the city's shore-line, and which formed one of the "villages" which were now hostile territory. A week ago he would have had free passage anywhere in Tiger's Bay – sanctuary, too, for the asking – but not any more.

Galloway looked through the railings at the line of shops opposite, for a sight of the enemy. He knew exactly who the enemy were. They would be young and moving restlessly about in groups of three or more. If they did halt for any length of time, it would only be to take up the classic stance, propped against the nearest wall, like some squad of one-legged teenage veterans. Making a great show of their smoking, their spitting and slogan-writing, nevertheless they carried back information. Galloway knew this. He also knew that they would be alerted on the instant by the sight of someone of their own age group, and with hair as short as their own. He watched and waited patiently until he felt convinced that he had nothing to fear from that quarter, then he moved swiftly out through the gates.

There was a bus-stop fifty yards ahead and he sweated until he reached it. A painted wooden shelter was nearby, its single bench occupied by more pensioners from the park. He squeezed himself in among them, all his former fine manners jettisoned. They shuffled their feet and rattled their sticks, but he bore their ill-temper and their reek of pipe tobacco and peppermints until a red double-decker pulled up. He bounded on to its lower deck, and was sitting inside behind the driver's back, before it had pulled out and was on its way to the suburb he was seeking.

Not far from his destination there was a nasty moment when a mob of schoolboys fought their way on board. Galloway sank in his seat as they clattered upstairs, for he had noted glances

coming in his direction as the bus had arrived at the stop opposite
the school. He knew the place well. It had long been on one of
Billy Bonner's many lists because of its reputation as an academy
for young terrorists. He felt glad he was not now sitting among
these same apprentice bombers on the upper deck, but when the
time came for him to get off, he found, to his dismay, that at least
a dozen had chosen the same stop. He was already on his feet and
by the door. They hemmed him in. They didn't look like
schoolboys, as he had known such. Their great hands and wrists
stuck out from their stained blazers, with the unpronounceable
name on its badge, their boots and shoes seemed reinforced for
some violent purpose, they smoked, swore and jostled. It wasn't
the first time Galloway had the nightmare feeling that this town
was being swamped by some monstrous birth explosion that had
taken place in the early sixties. He managed to jump off first,
however, and crossed behind the bus.

In his anxiety to get away, he was almost knocked down by a car
going in the opposite direction. The driver rolled his window
down, and abused him in a countryman's leisurely vernacular.
Galloway lowered his head while trembling with rage. It was hard
to keep Hyde in check at a time like this, yet he must do so, he told
himself. At all costs he must do so, if he were to survive the
course he had set himself this day and the next and perhaps the
next, until the revenge he had promised himself fell to him like
the ripest fruit he would ever taste. This bitterness in his mouth
at this moment only served to make that ultimate plum the
sweeter.

Behind him there were catcalls. The louts on the pavement
were enjoying his distress. He couldn't have attracted their
attention more if he had waved a red, white and blue flag – he
knew already they had sensed his allegiances only too well. He
managed to find a break in the traffic and, gaining the opposite
side, walked rapidly off in the direction the bus had come from,
hoping it would put them off. But when he looked over his
shoulder, he saw the pack strung out on the road, making a game
of dodging the traffic. The clamour of car-horns made him shake
anew, not from fear – another time he might even have enjoyed
facing these young hyenas, with or without the dagger in his boot
– but because he knew he could not afford any confrontation and
must avoid it, even if it meant further humiliation.

And that seemed unending, for now he began to walk very fast, in a parody of one of those stringy men in vest and shorts, the clowns of the athletics world. The shouts behind were getting louder. A stroller on the far side of the road stopped to watch the spectacle, as though it were an everyday occurrence for someone to be hunted in broad daylight. Galloway clenched his teeth. *Only give me time to get my job done first, that, at least.* He heard running feet; broke into a jog himself, still keeping to the fiction of someone out training for the good of his health.

Ahead was a turning to the right; he took it without breaking stride and found himself in a long tree-lined avenue stretching towards a distant but as yet unseen junction. His breathing was now troublesome; should he make a stand, he asked himself, back against one of these trees? There would be no refuge for him in any of the houses he was passing, that was certain. As he ran now, it came to him that these same houses, this avenue with its thick dark hedges of evergreen, seemed familiar. There was a gate he recognised, a front door painted brown, he even knew the pattern of the carpet inside that covered the stairs. A strange urge came over him to go through that gate and ring the bell, just as he had done on a night not so long ago. He passed the street-lamp he had shot at for amusement. A ragged collar of glass still clung to the top of its standard. It surprised him that nothing had been done about that.

And then in the distance he saw a group of figures. His vision was blurred, they stayed hazy for a very long time. Even the trees weren't slipping past as they had been.

There was a noise overhead; an army helicopter came low on its sweep across its quadrant of the city. It seemed to hover for a moment, as though those inside wanted to enjoy the sport taking place below. Galloway looked up at the bulging khaki belly; Perspex gleamed and dazzled. He stumbled, and when his sight cleared he was much closer to the figures ahead. They were waving at him – or so he thought – and they were wearing school blazers. Then something struck him, a stone; it fell at his feet, and in a moment, the air was filled with missiles, curving high to land about him on the roadway. He ran, ducking all the way, towards the crowd of rival sixth-formers now returning fire. They ignored him and, straightening up, he kept on walking until he had left them and their street-games far behind.

It was now lunchtime. It must be, he decided, if all these young ruffians were loose to roam abroad. His watch had been taken from him at his "rompering", so he looked up at the sun instead. It barely broke clear of the trees. Still, it would climb no higher today, that seemed certain. When he came to a row of shops, he went into a Spar and bought himself a pack of frankfurters from the cold shelf. He also asked for a large cardboard box. The chill, uncooked meat, tasting of brine, slid into his mouth, and he bit each section through with great, almost childish relish.

Then he continued on his way, holding the box out in front as though it were filled with groceries. Delivery boys, in such a neighbourhood, he had reasoned, must surely be a common sight. This box would be the passport he needed. But, when he reached the address he sought, he was surprised at once to see that it was a large house, set back from the road, and not the block of flats he had held in his head. He hesitated outside the gates, at a loss. The empty box seemed suddenly ridiculous. Could he have misheard the telephone operator and the number, and – or – the avenue she had given him? He now regretted bitterly having put the receiver down with such eagerness. He should at least have asked her to repeat the address. His stomach felt queasy, he thought of those raw lumps of foreign sausage lying there unchewed and resisting digestion. At the same time his brain was working at full pressure. He mustn't loiter here, with or without his box, it told him; that was imperative.

Feeling ill, he forced himself to proceed through the gates and up the short drive towards the red brick villa, with its air of faded grandeur. But as he came closer he noticed that the curtains on all of the windows were different, and then he saw the row of bell-pushes set into the wall beside the closed front door. His sickness began to leave him. He climbed the steps. *Harding*, he read, on a nameplate opposite the number nine. He looked around carefully before pressing the bell, waited, then pressed it a second and a third time. Holding his head close to the door for the sound of its distant peal, or even a footstep within, he could hear nothing. This was something he hadn't bargained for. He had rehearsed in his mind every detail of his meeting with this girl, all the little politenesses he had found so easy with the telephone operator, until he had gained an entrance to her place; then, with the door closed, and he trembled, thinking about it, Mr Hyde would at last be allowed to come into his own. Mr H. had been patient far too long; he deserved some fun.

Galloway stepped back and looked up at the high russet front

150

of the mansion. There was no sign of life, not even a car in the drive at his back, nothing. It came to him that this was a dead house during the day, but, as he was about to move round to its rear, hoping for an open window there, at least, his eye lighted on a small metal grille beside the bells. He had seen such a thing once before, and remembered the sound a voice makes coming from it when the magic number is pressed. So he began working his way down from the top floor; cunning told him the further away from the front door the better it would be for him. All twelve he pressed, waiting with patience between each for that click and then that weird crackling to follow, but nothing. He stepped back to look up in case a curtain twitched, but no movement caught his eye.

And then a voice did speak, it could have come from anywhere inside that vast place, from any of the numbers, but now it was issuing from the square pierced plate a foot away. Galloway pushed his cheek close. He held his breath.

"*Who is it?*" the voice repeated, a female voice, elderly, nervous, and no wonder, thought Galloway, all alone in that house of the dead.

"It's the man from the gas, missus! Here to read the meter!"

His voice rolled out alarmingly in the afternoon quiet. Silence. These old ones, he thought, regretting his action already – all she has to do is lift the phone, but then, as in answer to a prayer, mechanism whirred, and the door gave before him. He stepped in smartly, without his cardboard box, for that he no longer needed, and pushed the heavy door closed behind him. The whirring stopped, and it was like being in a tomb.

His heart beat. He stood in a big square hallway, a staircase ascending straight before him, what light there was filtering down from a grimy, cracked dome high overhead. There were two doors to his right, two to his left, and underfoot, an expanse of tiles, chequered, rugless and noisy, he felt bound. A vast depression weighed him down quite suddenly. This dusty, airless place, the circulars kicked into a corner behind the door, the wallpaper in tatters – what was he doing here? He thought of the sun, not that watery imitation outside, but the one he had promised himself, full, and as hot as a furnace. A man could find ease in heat and light like that, beachcombing by day for the barest necessities. Now he chafed at the slowness of this task he had set himself to complete before he could set out for those tropic climes.

He took his boots off, and, holding them and the dirk which had rode there, he tiptoed across the black and white tiles to the stairs. Then he halted at the thought of something, and retraced his steps, going to each of the doors in turn, to stop and listen. He could detect no sign of life, except a bird in a cage in number three.

On the first floor he repeated the performance. Again he could hear nothing. Up he mounted the next flight of stairs and went straight to number nine, the girl's room. The door looked no different from any of the others. He put his ear close to the jamb, half hoping for the slightest sound that would tell him luck had swung his way again but, beyond the wood, life seemed extinct, except for the mice, the woodworm or the cockroaches that lived under the bath.

On the floor above he halted, stunned, for he distinctly heard voices. They came from number eleven. He crept closer. A man's voice said, "Some more tea, mother?" and the reply followed, "Just a little, dear boy ... is this China or Indian? I suppose I really should know by this time, but then perhaps even my taste buds are going the way everything else is these days." The man laughed in a strange, artificial way, and then the sound simply faded away. Galloway heard a click, and realised that it was the radio he had been listening to.

Next moment he heard a movement from within, and another woman's voice said, "Now where's that bloody key got to?" but this was no actress, this was the old trout who had opened the front door for him.

Galloway ran on stockinged feet for the stairs and kept going down until he felt the chill of the hall tiles. He backed into a shadowy patch in the lee of the staircase and waited. Down she came searching in her handbag, still mumbling to herself. "Some of these days, girl, I'm telling you, some of these days, if you don't get a grip ..." There was the clink of empties from the holdall she was carrying on her arm, and Galloway realised she was a bit pissed. The cold bit through his socks as the pantomime continued all the way back and forth, back and forth across the hall to the front door. He was reminded of Duff and the manner in which he too would keep on searching, searching, until you felt obliged to do him some lasting damage. This old one would never know just how close she too had come to a violent assault from a person or persons unknown. Ned Galloway sweated in the dark afraid of what he might do if he looked down just once at the German dagger in his grip. Then the door slammed and she was gone.

Mr Hyde had waited long enough. Pulling on his boots, and to hell now with any noise he might make, the naughty one marched to the stairs and, taking them two at a time, raced up to the second floor, the naked blade held out in front like a provocation. Reaching the girl's door, he touched the keyhole once, for aim, then, with a single thrust of his leg, he kicked in the lock. There was little or no splintering, as he knew there would be, and no real sign on the outside that force had been applied. He pushed the door open, and walked into the flat. With care, he closed the door behind him, bending the lock back into position. Then, and only then, did he look about him.

She was not obsessive about neatness, this one, that was apparent. Either that or she had left the place in a hurry, but then, as he moved about, he noticed the coating of dust, the shoes kicked under the bed, the overflowing ashtrays, a tide-mark in bath and basin, the unwashed dishes, something rank in the pedal-bin, and he put her down for a slut. Like all women, he reflected; when they're not on display. The dressing-table and its array seemed to bear out his theory. He sniffed and sampled there, and then his attention was drawn to some photographs in stands on the mantelpiece. The same face appeared in all of them. He stared at the eyes, the dark helmet of hair, full mouth. She laughed back at the camera, at him – it was a studio-portrait. Then he carefully positioned the framed likeness, so that this woman, whoever she was, should watch everything he was about to do.

The destruction began slowly and in an almost precise manner. First, every drawer was turned out, and everything in it strewn on the floor. Then all the bottles and jars on the dressing-table were emptied over the ankle-deep drifts. Handfuls of powder, white, beige, pink, were flung like seed. He ran a lipstick back and forth across one wall until the brass holder bit into the plaster. Magazines and books were gutted, their pages fluttered. Then he opened the wardrobe and began slashing everything that hung inside, then flung the tatters, still on their hangers, on to the floor. He slithered on silk, he panted now, and the dropping talcum grains coated his wet face. From then on, the knife did the work, stabbing and cutting. He fancied it turned in his grasp like a dowser's rod, moving from one feat of havoc to the next, and he allowed it freedom, for each time that blade found a new mark, he felt the pressure inside ease. Each blow struck was for a remembered indignity. Faces became imprinted on the pillows and the cushions, and were gashed accordingly until the down flew like snowfall. Other faces replaced them, such a succession, it came to him, even at the height of the frenzy. Then, finally the blade seemed to be glutted, and he fell back on the mattress, run down like an old clock.

Lying there, watching the feathers settle, his own blood began to subside. He seemed to melt into the torn ticking. The feeling was almost sexual. He met the eyes in the photograph. They smiled provocatively and didn't waver, even when he unzipped himself. That look seemed to say, *come on, come on, I'm waiting.* His left hand touched silk and, from the floor, he drew up something pink and edged with lace. *Libra*, he read, in embroidered script ... then he groaned and the silk became suddenly damp. Ned Galloway fell back and drowsed then, and all the while the eyes from the mantelpiece smiled over him, almost tenderly.

When he awoke the light outside was beginning to go, and, for a moment, he felt panic that he might have overslept. With a jerk he sat upright on the bed and looked about him. He was surprised that the devastation was less dramatic than he'd imagined, disappointed too, but then, it was true that he'd had to desist from smashing things because of the noise. His progress had been a silent one, as silent as the knife lying beside him on the mattress.

He rose and, for the first time, with any real curiosity, began to prowl about the confines of the small flat; a living-room with a single bed, kitchen, a bathroom and toilet. Almost idly he turned things over on the floor with his toe, trinkets, torn photographs, clothing. Half of Humphrey Bogart's face remained on the wall. He decided to let him stay like that. In the bathroom cabinet were two almost full bottles of Valium, but then most of the population were on happy pills. And she liked her drop of drink too, that was obvious, from the dead men under the sink. He thought about this woman. In his own way he had got closer to her in the only way he knew, for in real life she would not have given someone like him the time of day. Now she would have to, whether she liked to or not. Already he was impatient for the moment when she would open the door and see him there waiting.

On top of the wardrobe was a suitcase with its old holiday labels still attached. *Palma Nova*, he read, and, in his mind associated the words with one of the photographs on the mantelpiece. A dago had his arm about her bare shoulders in a night-club, the flash contracting their eyes to pink dots. Galloway felt a twinge of jealousy and violently hauled down the the dusty case on to the floor. It was locked and curiosity made him take the point of his knife to it. Inside was an airline bag, and he shook out its contents. Two men's shirts, two pairs of underpants, a safety razor and soap, after-shave and a toothbrush – all new and still in their wrappings. There was also a tie, navy, to go with the paler shirts.

He sat looking at treasure trove. For a long time he did nothing else, smiling to himself, then took out his tin and rolled himself a perfect smoke. The pale fumes rose trembling in the late afternoon light, and soon the reek of scent was in retreat. *Boy oh boy*, he kept repeating to himself, *boy oh boy*. After the second and even more perfectly wrought joint, he went into the bathroom still murmuring his mantra, and cut down the plastic drying-line, laying it out in readiness on the bed alongside the tasteful tie. He revelled in his inventiveness, was even more delighted at his own reflection in the dressing-table mirror, for his hair was tufted white with down. Taking up a handful of lipsticks and thinner pencils, he began covering his face with stripes and whorls, until the result seemed not far removed from a work of art. He lay on the bed giggling, thinking of her face when she opened the door and saw his warpaint. Boy oh boy oh boy ...

19

THE MAN THEY CALLED Mr Wonderful sat in the only chair in the room, that was his right after all, and sipped from a glass of something clear, like water. He was dressed for the golf course and Billy Bonner knew that afterwards clubs would be hoisted from the boot of the maroon XJ-S standing in the car-park, and a round, or rounds played with influential friends. Afterwards. The word sent sweat trickling down his back, for Billy Bonner was expecting the worst.

Now he stood just inside the door, facing the man who had summoned him with such secrecy to this distant hotel room. Outside a rich deep voice laughed suddenly and others joined in from the terrace below. Self-pity swamped the short man in the business suit and that in itself, he realised now, was a further humiliation.

"The window." The words were undoubtedly a command, and he moved swiftly as though eagerness might somehow appease and the sliding panels kissed and met, the room on the instant becoming a dead place. Turning, he glanced down at the neat, oiled back of the head and, like a schoolboy, he found himself grimacing.

Then the voice murmured, "I'm not happy, not happy at all," and it had begun. "We had an understanding, you and I. A business arrangement, pure and simple. Now I find that has been put at risk by what has been happening on your side of the house. A sleeping-partner, I shouldn't have to remind you, should be allowed to stay in that state, when he's paying for the privilege."

He poured another measure from the bottle by his side. There was a swift, releasing hiss of bubbles, but Bonner couldn't make out what was on the label. For some reason he was suddenly curious, felt the urge to enquire, anything really to delay what might be coming next.

"Meeting here today is an indication of just how serious the situation has become. Almost out of hand."

"I don't think –"

"That's been the real trouble all along."

Bonner felt like loosening his tie. Beneath its formal suiting, his body seemed to be simmering in its own juice. The golfer in the chair regarded him with disinterested eyes. "Now, tell me," he asked, "just how close are you to finding this man – if at all?"

Billy Bonner did loosen his tie then, pulling the silk down into a hard, tight knot. "Jesus, it's hot in here!" he gasped.

"It's hot everywhere. An Indian summer, I think is what it's called, but then you've been far too preoccupied to notice the weather much – I trust."

"Look –" He paused, needing to call this man by name, but couldn't, not by his nickname, and certainly not by his real one, so well known it made him choke even to think of it. "Look, he can't last out much longer. How can he? This is only a wee place. It's only a matter of time."

The other shook his head. "Wrong. Every day, every hour this man's at large makes him more of a threat. When you came to me at the start of this whole episode, you assured me then that he posed no problem, no *threat*. Now he is. So what has changed, or, more to the point, what has gone wrong? Let me tell you. Instead of disposing of him at the outset, as you should have done, you proceeded to lead him around like a chimp on a chain, for your own amusement. Your vanity got the better of you. In other words you, my friend, cocked it up."

Bonner was shocked by the phrase, in spite of himself. Coming from such lips, it sounded like the worst profanity. He was also shocked that so much seemed to be known about his own affairs. He distinctly smelt betrayal, and that made him reckless. "If you don't like the way I'm handling things –"

The man in the chair laughed, a short mirthless bark. "You're a comedian as well, I see. You always did strike me as someone in the wrong line of business."

Billy Bonner felt his eyes sting. Why should he have to tolerate this, he asked himself. But the answer was plain, as plain as the difference between them must be to any eye, one upright and stiff in a suit with a waistcoat, the other, seated, easy, elegant in yellow cashmere and plaid pants.

The man they called Mr Wonderful observed the toes of his Oxfords, and, in a new and softer tone, said, "Business." He repeated it, and on his lips the words seemed to take on an almost sacred quality. "Business runs this place," he said. "Business *men*. Not politicians or even governments, but people like me. *Us*, I might have said at one time, for I did have hopes that you too might have joined our ranks." Billy Bonner felt a deep and sudden sense of deprivation. He stared at the carpet. "People believe everything they read in the history books. You must have noticed that, but you won't find *us* there. However, take it from me, behind every single event of any importance – ever – someone was calling the tune because he was in charge of the finance."

Billy Bonner thought that he had never heard anything quite so undeniable and it only made his unhappiness worse. He wanted another chance, oh, how desperately he needed that. Like a worshipper, he raised his eyes to the oracle, but the oracle no longer dispensed comforting truths. The tempered steel in the voice had returned, and he felt like an errand-boy once more.

"Our friend, who gave you the slip, what about his family?"

"Family?"

"Yes, you must have checked that out, surely. And I don't mean the ex-wife and the kiddy across the water."

Bonner blinked rapidly. This was news to him. He struggled hard to catch up, managing to say, "No one's been near his father, if that's what you mean. You can depend on that."

"Good. That does reassure me. Next question then. What about his little friend?"

This time the other didn't even attempt to hide his astonishment.

158

The man in the chair spoke slowly, as though to a child. "The Jock. Number one boy. Remember?"

"Galloway?"

"If that's his name."

"What's *he* got to do with it, for Christ's sake?"

"Plenty, if not everything, from what I've been able to piece together – from other sources." He smiled apologetically.

"Are you trying to tell me that Ned Galloway did a deal behind my back? With the big fellow? No way. No way."

In his agitation, Billy Bonner began pacing about the room. The man in the chair followed his movements with an amused smile on his face as though it was a clockwork toy he had set in motion.

"Your vanity is showing again," he murmured.

Bonner swung round. "That wee Scotch bastard is a back number, take it from me! Do you hear? We gave him something to remember us all by. A souvenir to take back home with him on the boat. He won't come back here again in a hurry, you can bet on it." He permitted himself a snort.

Mr Wonderful stood up and the action was so unexpected that all Billy Bonner's wrath leaked away in the same instant. The man who was dressed for the sporting outdoors seemed to tower above him shutting out the light. Those wide shoulders, the flatness of the midriff, the legs in their Daks, powerful and set apart, all proclaimed his fitness to rule.

"Bonner," he said, and the sound of his own name used for the first time, was a further intimidation. "Bonner, you're a fool, and you're beginning to tax my patience. Sit down." He pointed to the chair he had just left, and obediently the other sank on to its still-warm tweed. "Now, don't interrupt me. Listen, and benefit by what I am about to say. First of all, this Scotsman you tell me has gone home – hasn't. No later than yesterday he was in Mooney's in the centre of town, and didn't seem to care who knew it. At noon today, he was seen in the Antrim Road area. Unfortunately contact was broken shortly after, but we're pretty sure we can pick up that trail again. Even if we don't, we know where he goes to ground every night."

Billy Bonner's legs felt weak. It was just as well he had a chair under him in this expensive and overheated hotel bedroom. He felt very far from home now, and each time the word "we" was mentioned, he wondered whether it would even be wise to return there. God only knew what conspiracies had been hatching during his absence. Perhaps even this trip today . . .

"Now, the question we must ask ourselves is this," came breaking into his anxieties. "Why is this man still here, if, as you tell me, he's at risk? There can be only one answer to that. He's waiting for the right moment, the right moment when he can rendezvous with our other friend."

"I still can't believe – "

"Don't be such a bloody fool, man! The two of them have been in cahoots from the word go. It's obvious. What other explanation can there be?"

But Billy Bonner was searching his mind for the seeds of his betrayal. "What would Silver Steele give him that I couldn't. Tell me that, will you? He doesn't even own the clothes on his back, I tell you, has no friends, no money. He has *nothing* to offer, I tell you."

"That's where you're wrong. He has *something* – now – that can convert into cash. Assets that you handed to him on a plate when you took him on a conducted tour of your own set-up. Face facts, man, those two between them have enough gen on you now to clean up!"

Billy Bonner recalled with terrible clarity a scene not so long ago when he sat in another room with men like himself, listening to a voice coming haltingly from a tape-recorder. He remembered the questioning, those same angry suspicions he was hearing now as facts, but worst of all he remembered how he had felt almost sorry for the pathetic figure in the chair in the centre of that bare upstairs room. That was the moment when the treachery had started all right. He bowed his head, just as his betrayer had done then, and heard too the self-same tones of accusation – only *he* was now the one on the receiving end.

"A ready-made martyr, those were your words, and let the other crowd take the blame. Who's going to believe them anyway? Just think of the propaganda, just what the cause needs, etcetera, etcetera . . . But now, alas, our martyr-to-be is loose and knows enough to make the shit stick to a lot more of us than just you and yours."

Once again the obscenity jarred. Billy Bonner brought his knees together almost prudishly. He tried to say something in his own defence, but the man standing over him made a chopping motion with his hand.

"Don't waste your breath, and my time!" he barked. "The longer those two are out there, the more dangerous they become. Do I need to draw you a picture?" Then he sighed, as though he had exhausted himself. His voice became quieter, more thoughtful. "My friend, there's too much at stake here. Believe me, much, much more important things than private wars. Don't go grubbing about in the dung-heap of the past, like so many of the others in this part of the world. All I can tell you is this, there's something big in the offing, a change from top to bottom coming – soon – and, when the dust settles, loyalties won't be forgotten, I promise you. Don't miss the boat, whatever you do."

Billy Bonner noticed that the eyes had glazed over. It was the only thing that marred the effect the words were having on him, for he felt he could sit listening to this man speaking in this way for ever. But then the eyes found their focus again, were bright, unwavering as before. "The joke is, of course, that the man's days are numbered anyway. How long did that contact of yours in the hospital say the doctors had given him?"

"Three to six months at the most."

"And he knows that?"

"No. We got him out before they had time to tell him."

Mr Wonderful smiled. "Dying on his feet, and doesn't even know it. Unless of course the papers get wind of it, or the box. Yes, they might well leak it, those bastards, just to make him give himself up." He looked at Bonner. "No need to go on, do I?"

Billy Bonner rose unsteadily to his feet. He felt eager now, renewed for the fray, despite his nervous state. "I know where that bastard Galloway puts his head down. That's where we'll nail him, this very night. And then we'll get the pair of them. I'll handle it personally."

The other seemed to be holding back a smile but, nevertheless, he patted Bonner on the back reassuringly, while steering him to the door. "Good. Good man," he murmured. "I'm glad we've had our little chat. One last thing, however. From this point on, I'm afraid you're on your own. I don't know you, have never heard of you, you don't exist, as far as I'll be concerned. Nothing personal, you understand, merely expediency, because of the times we live in. Good luck and goodbye." There was no shaking of hands.

Outside in the corridor the Muzak pulsed, and Billy Bonner felt unsure of his steps in the dim lighting. Before he set off down

161

that long and lonely journey to the lifts, he righted the *Do Not Disturb* sign on the doorknob, out of some odd impulse of deference. As he bent over the gilt card on its cord, he heard the phone ring beyond. He found himself stooping to listen.

The man within laughed, and said, "My dear Gerald! And how's Kirsty? And your good self? *Me?* Couldn't be better . . . In the pink . . . Look, why don't I fly up in the Piper? Tonight . . . Of course. I'd love to get in a bit of shooting over the weekend . . ."

Billy Bonner walked quickly off down the corridor, feeling, for some reason, slightly sick.

20

He was back in the Compound, in the Drying-Hut, among the hanging laundry and everywhere he turned faces were peering out, grinning through steam, and when he looked at what they were all so taken with, he saw that it was a couple naked on the floor, a man and a woman, starfish limbs on the damp tiles, deep in the throes of passionate love. He wanted to warn them, to cover up their shame, but found he couldn't make a sound or move.

Beside the writhing pair lay their clothing thrown off in heat. He felt he recognised a scrap of something, a gaudy pattern; there were other things too, the cast of the man's body, for instance, the way his hair lay low on his nape. On one bicep, the left, was a small tattoo, a shield, legend almost obliterated, but he knew that date, the name of the famous battle, he remembered too the pain the blue-tipped needle had made jabbing away in that back room in Kuala Lumpur.

The man on the sweating tiled floor was *him*, the woman bonded to him, damp flesh on flesh, was Nan, but she seemed oblivious of the grinning gallery. He kept trying to alert her – they were getting bolder with every moment, but the manner in which she pinioned him made it impossible. Her mouth was clamped to his, he felt the pith slowly leaving him. All about, the watchers' faces swam in and out of vapour. He tried to signal mutely to them to have some decency, to leave the two of them in peace. After all, he knew these men, they respected him, but then he saw one of them much clearer than the rest. It was Billy Bonner, leather jacket glistening, a colossal smirk on his face. He had something in his grasp, something thin and silvery, he held it out before him. The man on the floor tried to pull away from its bulbous, meshed head, a wire leading back to where two discs revolved slowly among the feet of the watchers. But he was powerless as, closer, closer, the thing kept coming until he could make out the fine coating of moisture on its metal. He watched it the way he might watch a snake. Now it was close enough to pick up the sound of their labouring bodies, their breathing, to be relayed back to that whirring little box of tricks. But still it kept on coming, as though nothing could stop or satisfy it. He wanted to scream, to beat it back, before it left its imprint on him, and then, finally, he was crying out and he was awake and awash in his own sweat, half on, half off the camp-bed.

Sitting up in the middle of his dusty cave, he peered into corners for a glimpse of faces, but all was as it should have been. Yet he still could not quite believe it. He pulled and prodded his damp flesh, searching for the place where metal must have seared him. Pain there had been, nothing could persuade him otherwise, nightmare or no nightmare. It was what had shocked him awake. But he could find no trace, no mark. So now he lay back and waited for some sort of ease to return.

He thought of the woman in his dream. *Nan, not just a woman.* He said it to himself, angrily almost, but without real conviction. Why fool himself, things were much too desperate now for that, and he had decided to go his own way, not hers, no matter what she might believe. That moment of betrayal he had anticipated had finally arrived. It was why he had been so careful to hold back a part of himself all along. A little cold corner roped off against all comers.

He thought of her, what she might be doing at this time, alight with preparations for their adventure together, for, despite what she kept on saying about her no-nonsense side, he knew she really saw it like that – their adventure. This woman, nudging forty, despite her share of batterings, still remembered something from a girls' paper about a hunted man and a beautiful young courier who had led him through danger to safety on the last page.

But then, to be honest, didn't he have one of his own, a companion yarn – hero named Ned or Tom or Jim, some such simple thing, and he had escaped, hadn't he, from his bastille, evading pursuit with the help of this self-same girl, until, offered the choice of freedom, he had turned it down. *I must go back, can't you see that? They are still my comrades, nothing can or ever will alter that. My so-called crime is their crime. We are all bound together by our life in that place. My destiny is tied to theirs, until that day when together, as one, we will smash our way out, glorious band of brothers, and nothing will stand in our way. This country will be ours once more, and we will rule it well and wisely this time. Not like before. Right is on our side, after all, and who can gainsay us* . . . And such-like guff.

Our pulp-hero sat up in his bedclothes and shivered. Grey light was seeping through the drawn curtains, the birds were in full cry, yet he knew all the world was still fast asleep. Except for insomniacs, and the likes of him – and that held self-pity, that single phrase. It showed the direction his thoughts were leading him, back down once more into that pit where you lie curled up in your own filth. He had climbed out, remember? He struck himself with clenched fist, as though to remind, and at the same time punish, that part which betrays so easily. He must never allow it such power again.

When he had fallen out of the car, instead of being an act of will, that too had been mindless. Only he knew that, of course, but it was all that mattered. Since then he had been bundled back and forth like . . . his mind reached for, then fastened on, that makeshift object they used to boot about on waste-ground, made from rags or newspapers, until it disintegrated. The image was distressing, yet a necessary one. He looked at his clothes heaped on the solitary broken-backed chair in the corner. Yes, he had become like that all right.

He watched the window, noting how the light was beginning to take on a warmer tint. The birds too had quietened, as they always seemed to do after the early excesses of the dawn chorus. He had no way of telling the time. Nan had promised to leave him her big man's watch, but they had both forgotten about it. He thought of how pale and vulnerable the skin must be under that heavy metal. She had kept it on all the time they were making love. He could hear its tick coming and going, as they moved their bodies on the open sleeping-bag. If she had left it with him, its sound would have been a constant reminder of her. When he stirred inside the bag now, wafts of her scent came to him, but only every so often. He played a game, holding himself immobile to seal off all such reminders. Later, when he made his move, when he gave himself up, it would be no longer a game, he knew that.

Stiff as a crusader, he lay staring at the buckled ceiling. He thought of the rusty nails up there holding the boards to the rafters gradually slackening with age and corrosion, the worm spreading, dry rot adding its own methodical encroachment to the process of ruin. All would come down in time, to lie in a jumble of planks and pre-war patterned linoleum, until, termed an eyesore, it would be carted off to the local dump. Someone might come along, salvage the better timber, build something of their own – another weekend shack perhaps?

Into his imaginings swam a distraction. At the bottom of the bag, bunched, close to his feet, he could feel something. Reaching down, he gripped a handful of fine material, drew whatever it was up to the light. Before he saw it, however, he recognised by its scent that it was hers, some scrap of a garment. He spread the silk with one hand, holding it up, such a tiny pair of pants, so frivolous too, for the likes of her. He brought it – the things – closer, inhaled her odour, their mingled scents. Had she left this deliberately, realising how potent such a souvenir must be, or was it just carelessness? A stab of jealousy took hold of him as he wondered in how many other beds similar mementoes had been found.

Then he felt a real pain, there was no mistaking it for anything in the mind. It fluttered rapidly and violently in his forehead. Sweat broke out on him. He felt chilled to the bone, and, sensing somehow that these were only the warning signs of agony much worse to follow, he crammed the ball of black silk into his mouth to prevent himself crying out.

21

THE BUS WAS EMPTY, had been since it left the city depot, first on the timetable that morning. On its front seat lay a pile of wrapped newspapers. The driver kept getting out to hurl them at the closed doors of newsagents. Galloway could tell he hated this part of the job by the way his neck flamed each time he pulled up. The presence of a single passenger watching his efforts may also have angered him. Anyhow, he was a surly brute, there was no need to go into it any deeper than that. Normally he would have enjoyed the spectacle of someone else's discomfiture, but on this occasion, Galloway felt nervous. He was depending on this man to set him down at his destination, a place unknown to him, a place beyond the city limits. The very thought of the country made him sweat. He had nothing of reference to console himself with, nothing solid, all he could bring to mind was hazy, greenish in colour, and stretching as far as the eye could see. And in the middle of it all Ned Galloway, not knowing what to do with himself if something cropped up. He felt certain something would too. So he kept his head well down below the seat in front, so that the driver might not notice him so much.

At the next stop he waited for the heavy roll to thud against the shop-front, but this time the driver carried it with him and into the premises. After a few moments, he came out and, instead of getting in behind the wheel, came walking up the passageway. He stopped at Galloway's seat and stared down at him, chewing steadily. In his fist was a chocolate bar and not until he had disposed of it did he speak.

"Your change," he said. "A fiver, it was, you gave me?"

"Yes, yes." Galloway jerked into speech. "Sorry about that."

The driver waved away all apologies with a sticky hand and counted out three notes and some silver. "Are you on a holiday?" he asked, looking down at the holdall on the seat.

"Yes, yes. A bit of a break."

"Best time of year for it, and you'll have the place all to yourself. Don't worry, son, I'll give you a shout when we get there," and he turned and walked back the way he had come.

The bus moved off and up through the gears, and the engine seemed somehow to sing more sweetly, as they sped past hedges and fields, and even they now had lost their frightening aspect. Galloway's eyes prickled with sentiment. He had become so used to having to fight for everything, fight everyone, seeing faces set against him, that his own looks had taken on a hard reflection of their own. Like a child, he tried to make out those same features in the ashtray on the seat in front, but the dented metal gave nothing away.

He lay back against padded plush, eyes closed. Yes, not many people would have come through the way he had come through. Not many people would have got this far, for a start. For a moment, everything seemed so clear to him, as though he was looking down on a field of combat pitted with traps. He could also see his own path across that treacherous ground, each turn and twist made at precisely the right moment. And the reason he could see all this now was because he was within touching distance of the prize. Sweet fruit for his fingers alone. Revenge is sweet, or so they said; but none of that concerned him any more. It was the contest, the twists and the turns, the task he had set himself, that made him go on with it. He felt a rush of pride and, looking up the aisle at the driver, who was whistling loudly now, he wondered just how he would react if he knew who his solitary passenger really was. He wouldn't be so pleased with himself, he'd bet on that, wouldn't be so damned fatherly either. If he knew where and what he'd been up to, what he had in mind right at this moment, maybe he wouldn't be so easy-going, so free with his little services.

Sitting there in the travelling bus, Ned Galloway invented scenarios of violence and retribution against all sorts of people who had harmed him in the past. It had become a habit with him, and only when his face began to heat did he try to switch them off. However, the images continued to rise, the sequences that unfolded – he said this, then he said that, then the other person did this, and then, and then . . .

"Your stop!" shouted the driver without turning his head, and the bus began to slacken speed.

Galloway was startled, he lurched to his feet, ducked low to stare out at the grey ribbon of sea-wall, the waves beyond and, on his own side, spaced bungalows slowing as they glided past. He ran up the gangway as the brakes went on. A burnished rail behind the driver's head stopped him.

"Is this it?" he asked hoarsely.

"The post-office is straight ahead. See?"

Again he ducked his head. A shop of some sort, what looked like a bundle of children's fishing-nets propped up outside. Shakily, like an old man, he climbed down with his blue canvas bag. The driver laughed a loud laugh and drove off. Further on, outside the shop, he stopped, and the roll of morning papers flew out in a perfect arc.

Galloway stood where he was until the high rear windows disappeared from sight. He hadn't mentioned anything about a post-office when he had asked to be set down at the start of the journey. Then he remembered that laugh as the bus pulled away, and he felt as though he might never be able to move again from this spot, might just stand there in the sun with his bag on the ground at his feet. It seemed inevitable, because he could think of nothing else to do; his brain had seized.

A piercing cry from overhead made him crouch down. A great dirty-white bird flew low at him, or, so it seemed, then perched on the wall opposite. Its beak was yellow and hooked, its eye glittered in a head turned and held rigidly in profile. Galloway looked into that eye, looked deep, saw nothing there but his own downfall, if he didn't pull himself together.

"Fucking *seaside*! Fucking *country*!" he screamed, and the gull rose slowly as though tethered invisibly to the stones of the wall. He stooped for a handful of gravel, but it broke free, sliding away at an angle off and out to sea. A gob of white splattered on the ground. He wished he had a gun.

He crossed the road and looked over at a thin curving band of shingle which stretched in either direction as far as the eye could see. Water hissed and bubbled directly below. He watched the yellow turbulence until his own head began to swim, then he sat carefully down on the low wall and rolled a smoke, concentrating on the tiny ritual, as if it might well be the most important thing he would ever attend to.

Only when he had taken his first deep pull did he dare allow himself to think about his situation. Post-office. What post-office? There wasn't one, shouldn't be one; at least, not on the mental map he carried with him. Not a shop even, for that matter, to confuse it with. Confuse. The word had an ugly ring to it. Confuse, deceive. Was that what the girl – the woman – had done? Sent him out here, all this way, deceitfully? He thought not. No, he had too much faith in his own persuasive powers. He had been too patient, much too skilful for that. A long night and part of the morning too going over and over the same ground, from the first outright denials, to the final sobbing confession, and then the details after that, a dozen more times, to detect variations. In the end there weren't any. He had the map in his head by then, the one she had given him. The sound of a filling bath. So simple, but that's what broke her. In the next room, she was tied to the chair, and he let the sound of the taps do his work for him. He didn't even have to switch on the hairdryer as an extra inducement. Imagination. Most people, he found, had enough of the stuff when the situation called for it.

Now, with his nerves steadier, he went over those precious details he had wrung from her. A name, to start with, for the bus-driver, then landmarks for himself: a gospel-hall with a green roof, a rock at sea, bleached with droppings, an arch carved out of the cliff, water dripping, summer and winter, then beyond, a caravan site on the shore and, opposite the caravans, six at most, journey's end or *Bella Vista*, to be precise, the name in white pebbles set into twin pillars.

Bella Vista. He repeated it softly to himself. It soothed the more you said it. *Bella Vista.* He thought of people sitting under awnings, tall glasses in their hands, floating slices of fruit. He felt thirsty and looked in the direction of the shop. He had to make a start somewhere and the sooner the better, for it was clear by now that the bus-driver had deliberately set him down at the wrong stop. Again he heard that parting laugh, the laugh of a fool who has found someone more foolish than himself. Galloway sighed and reached down for the holdall. Another score to be settled, he told himself.

All the way to the shop – post-office – his former nervousness was returning. He felt isolated on the bare bright stretch of road, his feet seemed to be making more noise then they should. A woman weeding in her front garden shifted laboriously on her knees to stare after him. By the time he had reached the shop the back of his T-shirt was clinging to him.

He took a can of Pepsi from the open freezer and handed his money to the girl behind the counter without a word. She smiled slyly at him and he felt startled. Then, he recognised it for what it was, one member of the tribe putting out signals to another. Emboldened, he allowed his eyes to travel about the packed interior, the lotion and sunglasses, buckets, spades, a revolving tower of postcards and, in one corner, the grille that marked off the postal side of the operation. He looked at the postcards and there, in the middle of a coastal view, was the arch.

"How far are we from this place?"

She took the glossy card from his fingers almost tenderly, while he stared at her steadily. "Not far. About a mile or so. You'll be able to see it, when you get to the next bend."

"Bend? Which direction?"

She looked at him in surprise and he realised she would remember what he'd said. "I'll show you," and they walked out into the sunshine.

He followed her pointing hand, more road, the bungalows thinning away to empty fields, the sea-wall drawing the eye to a point where it disappeared into the hillside. It seemed a great distance to Galloway. Already he had a picture of himself toiling all that way, a lonely speck on the landscape, the way he must appear to that seabird.

The girl called out to him, "Do you want this?" waving the card from the doorway. He was yards away. He looked back at her standing there in her white overall. He made no sign that he had heard.

He resumed his journey, brows clenched in concentration, for nothing must stand in his way now. A feeling that time was running out oppressed him as well. The sun seemed to be speeding to its highest point overhead, yet the watch on his wrist told him it was still only a little after ten. It was *her* watch, and it felt strange to him, either too loose or too tight, depending on how much he adjusted the strap; strange, too, to be wearing something belonging to her. All the time she was in his power, helpless like that, there had not been the slightest touch of feeling on his part, but now, for the first time, he thought of her in a sexual way – of something he had denied himself needlessly. His imagination, too, played with her and the man he was hunting. Nothing had held them back from their games together, no, they had gone straight ahead, he didn't have to be told that. With a sudden fury, he swung the holdall at the wall as if to punish them for their selfishness.

At that instant a car came towards him, just an ordinary, pale-coloured saloon, but it struck dread into him all the same. He felt certain that the driver would pull up suddenly a mile or so further on, come back for him, if he didn't manage to reach the arch in time. He began to walk faster. If he had only travelled by some other means there would have been no need for this panic. If he had taken a taxi, for instance, hired a driver, his original idea, because he had his windfall by then, enough to pay for a dozen such, three hundred and twenty-six pounds, to be exact, drawn out of her building society the previous day. The proof of it was there in the pass-book. But then he thought of road-blocks, they were routine and regular everywhere now, so he knew he must think again. And so it came to him, the obvious, yet at the same time the masterly, for who would ever expect an assassin to go by Ulsterbus.

And then that grinning ape of a driver had spoiled the perfection. He had a brief but glorious image of a head-on collision just around the bend ahead, a fat frame pinned in the wreckage. He would look down at him in his agony, smile, then pass on, whistling.

The little fantasy seemed to speed his passage for here, suddenly, he was turning the long-awaited corner. A bay stretched below, bathed in bright sunlight, replica of the one on the postcard. There was no bus lying on its side in the roadway but there was something more important, an archway cut in the headland that fell in a jumble of rocks into the sea. The road raced into the dark hole and emerged on the far side, curving past scattered bungalows. There were caravans close to the sea and a building larger than all the rest, with a bright, newly painted roof. Even at this distance Galloway could read words on it, *Seek And Ye Shall Find, Saith The Lord* – white against the green, as though it were a message for the eyes alone of someone up aloft. Galloway grinned.

"Hallelujah," he murmured, quickening his pace. "Someone up there loves me."

22

THE NAKED MAN on the floor had tried to curl up tightly in a ball, but it was plain to see he was the wrong shape for much success. It was plain to the other man in the room, the younger, stronger, fully clothed one. He now sat on the solitary chair, smoking, his eyes cold, while images of other losers kept passing through his head. Men with dogs and whips herded these before them, and he understood so clearly how they must have felt, the uniformed ones, the booted ones; though the history books all pretended not to. He felt angry at the widespread lying that went on about something so clearly manifest.

Without taking the cigarette out of his mouth, he rose then, and kicked the other man a second time because of it. The man on the floor groaned, his eyelids fluttering. The dark scrap of something he had been twisting in his grasp fell to the floor. It looked like a piece of silk.

"Don't go snuffing it, now, big man. Do you hear me?" But the big man was trying to focus all his attention on where the kicks were coming from. Everything was a milky blur to him. He couldn't understand why it should be, how the pain in his head, the pain that had made him lose consciousness in the first place, should have such an effect.

The voice continued out of the haze. "A merry little dance, that's what you've led me. Over hill and dale. But nobody ever gets the drop on this chiel. Remember that. Do you hear me?"

The pitch had risen. The man on the dusty floor could also tell that the presence had changed position. Accordingly he moved his own head jerkily in search of it.

The other stood looking down with contempt on this poor pit-pony, was carried back once more to that earlier epoch where he might have strolled about in black leather, disposing of similar refuse. From his right boot he drew up and out his beautiful avenging blade. It was living its time all over again.

The man on the floor caught the flash of steel and suddenly this bright point of light seemed to drive away the murk, returning everything in the room to a shocking clarity. He could see a standing figure in a bomber jacket too big for it, stained jeans. The face bore marks that hadn't been there before, also a grey, drawn look that accompanied lack of sleep. The man on the floor surreptitiously cupped nakedness, preparing to acquit himself at the slightest movement of the blade in his direction, but it didn't come. Instead, the dagger continued to be held up to the light, fondled almost idolatrously by the crop-haired one. It was as if he no longer existed and he took comfort from that, beginning to edge himself as unobtrusively as he could closer to the wall.

"Cold steel. Makes them squeal," and grinning at his invention, drew the thing a few inches in front of his own scrawny neck.

The naked man felt an even greater distaste towards this sick creature start to rise in him. It gave him the courage to croak, "So Bonner is still employing boy-scouts, is he?"

The other's rage was total. "This is *my* show, my very ain!" he shouted. The knife flashed up, then down, to embed itself in the rotting wood of the chair. There were flecks of white in the corners of his mouth. "Bonner's a ham-bone! I wouldnae use him for toilet paper!"

He grabbed hold of the bag he had brought with him. "Recognise this?" shaking it high in the air. The man on the floor pretended interest but his mind was really bent on the knife. If he moved now, could he get to it before the other dropped the navy holdall?

Then the manic figure in the leather jerkin was unzipping the bag, pulling its contents out on to the floor. He flung a shirt at the naked man, as if to clothe him, then another shirt, then underwear, then some toilet articles last of all. The hard edge of a cellophane pack caught the big man in the face, then fell in his lap. He saw that it held a razor and quickly covered it with his hand.

"Come on, come on, they're all your size. And this," he threw a tie at him. "Blue's your favourite colour now, isn't it?"

The man on the floor was at a loss, but tried hard not to show it. Perhaps this knife-man was crazed, but then again, perhaps not.

"You thought you were safe, didn't you? Thought nobody could ever sniff you out, but *I* did. *Me*. I worked it all out by myself. *Me*. With nae help from anybody. Only hindrance."

The man on the floor saw that suddenly there were tears in the other's eyes. He recognised the emotion. He said, "I find that hard to believe," and was surprised at his own coolness. The airline bag fell to the floor, and his chance for the knife had gone.

"I don't care two fucks what you believe, or dinnae believe!" But it was clear that he did.

The naked man grew even bolder. "Why are you doing all this?" He pointed at the knife, its blade a good inch in the seat of the chair. "What have *I* ever done to you?"

The other's mouth opened and both waited for the roar, but it didn't arrive. The two men stared at each other, the gaunt veteran and the stocky little battler who carried his bruises so proudly. For oh such a long time had he borne his grievances, they fermented within, a septic broth that was eating him up, but now, when it was time for all of it to come spewing out, he found he couldn't put the words together. How could he bring himself to whine like a schoolgirl about a broken trust, a bond growing between the two that the other had spurned when he had made his escape, leaving him to face the music.

The man on the floor, his back to the wall by now, sensed something of what was going on in the other's head. He spoke quickly before violence could solve the problem for him. "You're fighting for the wrong side. You've no quarrel with me. How can I convince you of that?"

"You can't."

"But I have to. Time is running out."

"For you, it is. If you only knew just how quick."

"Look around you, man. Listen to it. Smell it. Deals are being done. In the dark. Soon they'll not even bother to hide their dirty business. If a cancer like Bonner can come out into the open, think of all the others. The ones hiding behind their respectability, their seats on the board."

"You're barmy. That place has got tae ye."

"Listen to me, Ned Galloway. You have the chance to get on the right side for once in your life. Before it's too late. Do it. Join us."

"Us?"

"Yes. We're almost ready. When the time comes, and it will be soon, soon, we're coming out. Do you understand what I say? Help us to sweep all this filth away. For good. A clean sweep . . . New start . . ."

The big man fell back coughing against the wall of the shack. The other stood looking down at him. There was a bottle of mineral water on the window ledge near the folding-bed. He brought it across, putting it to the other's lips. Then he pulled it away. "You bastard, you're conning me! You're conning yourself too, if you believe all that."

"What else can the likes of us believe in?" came the tired voice, then, "*We* never had our revolution. *They* kept it from us. Our right."

There was silence in that terminal place. The two men faced each other wearily. The younger felt no supremacy any more. His legs ached, yet some vestige of pride kept him standing. An insect that must have entered the dead, airless place along with him when he had smashed the window, buzzed spasmodically then seemed to lose all fight as well.

He said, "You shouldnae have jumped out of the car on me like that."

The man crouched on naked haunches said softly. "I didn't. I fell."

A vehicle of some kind passed on the road outside. There must have been others, but it was the first to register. The hum dwindled until the sea sound gradually re-asserted itself once more. They listened to that with a kind of dulled wonderment.

Still on his feet, Galloway raised an arm to wipe away the sweat that had gathered on his brow, and, as he did so, the sleeve of his

177

jacket pulled back and the man on the floor saw the big watch, its metal strap loose, the blue-black dial, the information about diving depths in luminous script. He didn't need to be told such details, he had seen them for himself, had felt that chill circular imprint against his own skin, heard the passionless tick in the dark. He whispered, "Where did you get that?" and his voice was hoarse.

"Get what?"

"That!" pointing.

"This?" and, shaking it on his pale wrist, Ned Galloway laughed. "A souvenir," he said, with a wink. "A souvenir of a very nice time." He put the watch to his lips.

The shout the naked man gave startled them both. It seemed to shake this rotting structure itself, for a fine dropping mist of dust suddenly filled the columns of light from the window. The other's mood changed, the cropped head coming forward, the jaw jutting, and the eyes taking on their old dangerous glitter.

"Who do you think directed me here then? Eh? Tell me that, will you? I didnae fucking well use telepathy, ye ken."

"She'd never tell you a thing. Nothing!"

"You think not, do you? Eh? Look, friend, you've been ta'en for a ride. Shopped. Do you savvy?" And again he shook the watch as the proof of that betrayal.

The man on the floor stared at the moving metal. It seemed to blur, and once more he was back to his earlier state. Half-blind again, he raised himself, bare back rubbing painfully against the board wall, and out of the haze, from the point where the watch glittered, the voice continued. "She spilled her guts, I tell you. Nobody else knew about this place. I was at her flat. I stayed the night. Cosy. Just the two of us. Listen, she has this big mole —"

He launched himself at the flicker of light, at the voice, the blade from the razor she had packed for him his only weapon. Blood roaring in his brain, he slashed at where he imagined the grinning face must be, then he was grappled, the rough leather bruising, shocking to the touch. He recalled unarmed combat sessions on the exercise-ground, heard his own voice roaring out advice and admonition, yet all he could find of value now was the precept about protecting one's bare feet at all costs. Accordingly, he entwined himself about the other's trunk and legs, lifting his own soles clear of the floor.

His assailant roared, tried to shake him off, wanting to put an

178

end to all this by getting to the chair and the knife. Strangely enough, he felt no real personal danger; instead, a kind of regret at the undignified way in which things had turned out. He thought of that other man scrambling on hands and knees on his own stairs, and then he felt a burning pain in his cheek. It gave him both strength and the will to hurl this old man of the sea away from him, finally. He fell to the floor panting and staring up at him. Galloway put a hand up to his face and when he brought it away the hand was red, wet. A horror seized him, it was happening all over again, all over again. He held the hand out before him, as though it belonged to someone else. He could feel it start to burn, just like that other time. His own blood, he told himself, but he couldn't make himself believe it.

He looked at the man on the floor for an answer. He was getting to his feet, still staring in that strange fixed way. Now he was moving towards the chair, and Galloway watched in paralysed fascination his hands feeling the air. They missed their mark, fluttered for a moment, then closed on the wood. Then he had the knife. He was coming across the room towards him, his eyes straining, a man of half his weight, despite his height, completely naked, and his pubic hair was reddish in colour. It was somehow startling, that variance, and Galloway was still pondering it in half-hypnotised fashion when the other's outstretched palm touched his chest. He stood his ground, letting it happen to him and he wondered why he had let it happen, all of this. At any time he could have stopped it, but hadn't, couldn't somehow, even when he knew the hand on his chest meant that the other was steadying his aim. Almost lazily then he looked down and watched the point of his own knife going in cleanly and neatly at the slight upward angle that the training manuals recommend. There was no pain, just a warm damp sensation like bed-wetting. He put his arms on this man's thin naked shoulders, drew him close, wanting to tell him, oh, tell him so much, but all he could manage was, "Not worth it. A huer ... All of them ... huers ..." then the sound of someone panting harshly grew louder and louder until the room filled with it.

The prisoner heard the sound too, while he stood there holding up his strange dancing-partner. When he realised that it came from himself, only then did he very gently steer both of them towards the bed, to where he remembered it to be. The trailing legs came to a halt against its side, the rest of his burden he lowered on to the spread sleeping-bag. The prisoner straightened the limbs on the cool, shiny lining almost delicately, covering the hasp of the knife with a corner of the stranger's leather jacket. He smelt his scent – tobacco, stale food and sweat, his hand in passing brushing the erection that bunched the denim. Ultimate urge.

He dropped down then on to the floor. There was blood on one of his hands, drying rapidly. Stuck to the centre of the stain, he saw a small disc of pinkish paper. Whoever came to this room, to find a dead man, would also discover similar tiny scraps scattered in the dust. The puzzle of how confetti and a corpse could ever come to be together would stay with them long after they had left this place.

He looked at the caste mark on the back of his hand, remembering her laugh as the paper cascade poured over him. He had killed a man because of that laugh, echoing in his head as he went for the knife, keeping on and on even as he was pulling it from the wood, tracking the other's presence across the floor, finally pushing home the blade. Then it had stopped, and he was left alone with his deed. It was her laugh that had made him do what he had to do, not that earlier laugh, but the one he heard in his head, when the man he was to kill talked about her in that way and he had to die because of it, because he had been the one to convince him of her betrayal.

He felt lack of breath suddenly as though he had reached the end of a race, his thoughts carrying him on without respite, until that word had brought him up short. Betrayal. It sounded like something from a forgotten language. There were so many other words he would have to unlearn from now on, all those words he had been in the habit of using, for he hadn't the right any longer. He had killed for the *second* time. But it was the manner of this second killing that had changed everything. There was no explaining that away to anyone, especially to himself. He had forfeited all future rights, all future dreams, dreams he had constructed for himself and the others in that place of wire and guard-towers until it had become the only reason for getting through each day: all of that was at an end for him. He would have, could have no part in it any more.

The light was beginning to fail outside, he could tell, despite his eyes. He thought of the city and the street-lamps lighting one by one, his city, the city that had made him what he was. Old and cynical begetter, it watched its sons come, it watched them go. Despite dreams, he had been brought back down to the level of its streets, as it always knew he would.

In a little while, when his sight returned to him, he would rise, dress himself and go out to find a phone-box. He would dial the number printed there, and tell them where he was, and they would come for him. Perhaps they would lock him away apart from the others this time. He would have plenty of time to go over the things that crammed his head. That would be his sentence, for the city always made you pay for your dreams.

SOUR SWEET

Timothy Mo

An intriguing and finely written novel of the enclosed Chinese
community living at the centre of 60s London.
'Brilliant . . . classic comic scenes . . . an excellent book.'
Sunday Times
'Uncovers a vivid, densely populated city within the city,
whose inhabitants have an individuality and energy that makes
the surrounding English look very grey. More than a touch of
early Dickens . . . has a flavour all of its own.' *Observer*
'In SOUR SWEET Timothy Mo has brilliantly combined the
comic with the frightening.' *Daily Telegraph*
'The characters and atmosphere in SOUR SWEET are
enthralling, and Mo has a deliciously gingery sense of humour.'
The Listener

FICTION   0 349 12392 6   £2.95

GOOD BEHAVIOUR
Molly Keane

Behind the gates of Temple Alice the
aristocratic Anglo-Irish St Charles family sinks
into a state of decaying grace. To Aroon St
Charles, large and unlovely daughter of the
house, the fierce forces of sex, money, jealousy
and love seem locked out by the ritual patterns
of good behaviour. But crumbling codes of
conduct cannot hope to save the members of
the St Charles family from their own unruly
and inadmissible desires.

'An extraordinary tour de force of fictional
presentation . . . a masterpiece . . . a technically
remarkable work, as sharp as a blade . . . Molly
Keane is a mistress of wicked
comedy.'   Malcolm Bradbury, *Vogue*

'Excellent . . . Molly Keane brings it off
triumphantly . . . a distinguished
comeback.'   Piers Paul Read, *The Standard*

FICTION   0 349 12075 7   £2.95

Other titles available from ABACUS

NON-FICTION

YELLOW RAIN	Sterling Seagrave	£3.25 ☐
MEDIATIONS	Martin Esslin	£2.95 ☐
NAM	Mark Baker	£2.75 ☐
IRELAND – A HISTORY	Robert Kee	£5.95 ☐
THE MAKING OF MANKIND	Richard Leakey	£5.95 ☐
SMALL IS BEAUTIFUL	E. F. Schumacher	£2.50 ☐
GANDHI – A MEMOIR	William L. Shirer	£1.75 ☐
HITCH	John Russell Taylor	£2.75 ☐

FICTION

WHEN THE EMPEROR DIES	Mason McCann Smith	£3.95 ☐
THE RED COMMISSAR	Jaroslav Hasek	£2.95 ☐
A LONG WAY FROM VERONA	Jane Gardam	£2.25 ☐
FREDDY'S BOOK	John Gardner	£2.50 ☐
GOOD BEHAVIOUR	Molly Keane	£2.95 ☐
MADAME SOUSATZKA	Bernice Rubens	£2.25 ☐
A STANDARD OF BEHAVIOUR	William Trevor	£1.95 ☐

All Abacus books are available at your local bookshop or newsagent, or can be ordered direct from the publisher. Just tick the titles you want and fill in the form below.

Name _____

Address _____

_____

Write to Abacus Books, Cash Sales Department, P.O. Box 11, Falmouth, Cornwall TR10 9EN

Please enclose cheque or postal order to the value of the cover price plus:

UK: 45p for the first book plus 20p for the second book and 14p for each additional book ordered to a maximum charge of £1.63.

OVERSEAS: 75p for the first book plus 21p per copy for each additional book.

BFPO & EIRE: 45p for the first book, 20p for the second book plus 14p per copy for the next 7 books, thereafter 8p per book.

Abacus Books reserve the right to show new retail prices on covers which may differ from those previously advertised in the text or elsewhere, and to increase postal rates in accordance with the PO.